WARNIN〈

To give you an idea of what you'￼ ＿﹍ᴏ, I ask
that my family put this down first. Turn off your kindle.
If you don't, gatherings might be awkward.
There, I said it.
Content warnings are as follows – mentions of suicidal
ideation, graphic violence, graphic erotic scenes, dark
romance, dark psychology.
These are not your friendly neighbourhood fae and I
like my heroines twisted.

—Quinn Blackbird

SHADOW FAE
BOOK ONE

DARK FAE: EXTINCTION

BOX SET ONE of TWO
BOOKS 1 & 2

QUINN BLACKBIRD

other than the pure black nothing so thick and glossy that I remember thinking back then that it was as though the window was lacquered obsidian from the outside

I'd lived most of my life alone, but it was then that I felt it most. With so many dying around me, and all that I could face was the darkness on the other side of the window—an omen of what was to come to this world—I wondered then if it would be best to simply die along with everyone else in the flooded hospital room.

Alas, my luck meant that I survived it. I caught it, suffered for most of the wars that erupted between neighbouring countries (food shortages will drive just about anyone to violence) and the dark fae coming and the evacuations, then simply woke up one day without a fever. The next day, I could move. And on the third day, no one came to my bedside when I finally managed to call out for help.

It was on the fourth day that I was able to wander (or stagger) around the hospital and I realised that those who had survived—doctors, nurses, patients, whoever—had abandoned the place.

I'd tried the phone. Every phone I could find. Got no dial tone, it was just silence. I couldn't get in touch with anyone; not my mother, nor my father, not even that one girl, Natalie, from boarding school who might be considered a friend if being generous. In truth, there are no friendships among the rich, only pacts.

And I was left without alliances, in a world I didn't know, where things had happened that I knew nothing about.

It wasn't for weeks that I came across others—a surviving group—and learned all that I'd missed.

Needless to say, everyone I've ever known in the Before is presumed dead.

Most of the world is dead. We know that since the dark fae spread out around Europe first, left it mostly intact, then reached the farther ends of the world. With all the rumours drifting between surviving groups over time, one theme was constant—the dark fae were *burning* their way through the world back to us.

And they have reached us, leaving behind a world—cities, towns, villages, farms—completely decimated. Swarms of their armies have burnt our human world to ashes, and now it's all we can do to keep a day's distance between us and the nearest dark fae army. There aren't many survivors anymore, not with so many of the dark fae coming back this way, killing the humans they find, burning all of our histories.

There is no escaping them. No outrunning the inevitable.

We all know that, every single person in this group has accepted this glaring truth. But the question remained for a while—what do we do about it?

Waiting around to be butchered just didn't seem to be a popular option in our group. So we came up with a scrap of a plan.

In this kitchen, with the perfect vantage point to the street down there, an almost-finished homemade bomb tucked away in the corner, and some stray dark fae separated from their army and headed our way, we will go out with a bang.

That's what we're doing here.

We are here to fight.

And we are here to die.

THE DARK

First came the darkness, billowing out of Britain.

Then the world went quiet. Radios turned silent, planes fell out of the sky. Our technologies died.

Famine erupted through the world like a bomb, bloodying battlefields between countries

It was the plague, however, that wiped out most of our numbers.

My name is Coralie and I fell victim to that very virus. I was one of the few who survived.

But nothing—absolutely nothing—could have prepared us for what came next; *them* charging into our globe in their hundreds of armies, spreading across the world like a new darkness and plague combined...

The dark fae have come to finish what they started. They have come to end us.

I
NOW

I have almost died too many times to count. Most of us who have survived this long can say the same. Lives lived with bunches of *almosts* and *nearlys* and *not-quites*.

The last time I met my almost death was only a couple of days ago—if the concept of 'day and night' even exists anymore.

Since before the dark fae came to this world, their pitch-black air billowed out of the Scottish Highlands and rolled over the world. From above, nothing can penetrate the thick blackness that engulfs us—not the moon, the stars, the sun. We are lost in the nothingness down here with only the occasional weak torches to give us dusty light.

That darkness brought with it the loss of all that we knew. Technology, abundant food sources, sight, safety—all gone. And the black air brought so much more; *a plague*. One so rampant yet silent and wholly aggressive that, even though I was one of the very few to survive the virus, I still feel its effects in my body today.

The chills cling to my bones, my fingers tremble and twitch, and there is a constant pallor of my weak skin that—if I'm cut—bleeds for too long before healing. All mere echoes of the pain I once suffered for weeks, trapped in quarantine with dying patients littered in iron beds all around me.

Memories of those gruelling, torturous quarantine days haunt me. They come in flashbacks so vibrant that a violent shudder rolls through my body.

On a stuffy, torn couch, I wrap my arms around myself and bring my legs up to tuck my knees to my chest. I'm all balled up, resting my heart-shaped chin on my creaky kneecaps (symptoms of too-long walks through the rough cobblestone streets and paths of France's West).

I clench my hands at my legs to stifle the trembles taking root there. Cutting my dark-blue eyes (not the hue to stand out with blazing brilliance) around the crammed apartment kitchen, I see that sometime during my supressed memories, most of the small group has found sleep.

We reached the town of Tours—our torches illuminated the town signs on the main road a while back—no more than some hours ago, so I'm amazed that so many of us have caved to sleep already. It's like the traumas of this cold, dark world don't haunt them in the quiet moments, and as though out there, the dark fae don't pillage and burn and destroy in a never-ending burden of loathing.

And loathe us, the dark fae do.

Why else would they have waged war on us? These creatures that we knew so little of, beasts that we thought to be old tales spun by ancient peoples, utter myths—they came to our world, darkness and plague and war, to end us, all without us even having the slightest suspicion that the dark fae existed.

Well, joke's on us. And we are the punchline.

A bitter smile warps my face into something of a grimace. I bury my face into my knees, protecting my grim expression from those few of us still awake in the kitchen. Slightly, I shake my head at my own twisted sense of humour.

In a heartbeat, the smile is wiped right off my

freckle-dusted face. The trembling in my hands surges with a sudden vengeance. I flex my fingers, peeling them apart from each other then give them a good shake.

This gesture draws in a few glances. The two lingering stares come from a married middle-aged couple tucked in the corner of the room, pressed against chipped white-painted cabinets. I can make them out only due to the blue gas-flames burning on the cooktop. We lit them when we barricaded ourselves in here for a rest.

Any chance not to use up our torches is an opportunity not to be missed. Torches aren't all that difficult to find, it's the batteries you've got to look out for. It all comes down to them, and back when quarantines were popping up and the darkness caused evacuations to spring up all over the world, batteries were one of the things looted by most, and left behind in the so few.

At the reminder of the black world and early days, I look at the window. It's propped up above the sink, overlooking the street below, where medieval-faced houses line the cobblestone. A set of cheap metal-like blinds covers the window, but through the creaks and dents and gaps, I can make out the pitch-black air beyond the window.

The darkness came before the virus did, but it was in quarantine that I recall the true bone-deep terror of it.

My bed was tucked at an angle beside the panelled window. I spent my days staring out of it, picturing the grassy hills of Southern France that should have been there—and they were there, somewhere devoured by the dark air. But I didn't see a damn thing

2
THEN

The handful of dark fae strays coming our way isn't something we would have known if it weren't for the most recent *almost*-death I mentioned earlier.

Loudun, France is a commune about a day's walk from Tours, where we are now. It was in Loudun that we were hiding out, gathering supplies, getting some real rest (well, everyone else got some *zzz's* but I find it hard to sleep longer than twenty minutes at a time without the sudden terror of dark fae hunting us zapping through my body and jolting me awake). Good thing I wasn't sleeping that night, since I was the first to feel it—

The tremor.

It shuddered the floor of the grocer's shop, rattled the windows in their frames with the sounds of faint whispers, like wind whistling through cracks. At first, that's exactly what I thought it was—wind creeping into our dark space. But it was no breeze, no gush of air. It was the first symptom of what was to come: an earthquake.

It wasn't my first thought. Even when all twelve of us had woken up to the third surge of rattles whose violence increased with enough power to rain down dust from the panelled ceiling, no one suspected that we were about to be thrown into the midst of an earthquake, cracks in the earth beneath us.

I'm from the South of France, spent much of my time at our villa there, gone for those semesters at boarding school. I know my country. France doesn't get

earthquakes … at least not before the dark fae invaded us.

Now, there is little to recognise in this new world. Whether the earth is rejecting the invaders, the darkness, the loss of its original and wretched guardians, I don't know. All I know is that the earth is angry, and we wound up in the middle of its rage.

That day was a brutal one; more so than any I've ever faced before.

Mere rapid heartbeats after the third tremor, the entire group flew up in a flurry. Hands were snatching at duffel bags, clattering sounds of people fumbling with torches echoed out, the scuffs of boots scraped over the linoleum floor.

Everyone grabbed what they could, even with the ceiling dust turning to chunks of cardboard-like wood starting to rain down on us. One, the size of a half-torn torso, whacked me on the head, good and hard. The hit was enough to drop me to the floor like a sack of rice. But it didn't knock me out.

Dazed, I staggered to my feet, felt around in the shuddering shop for my things. I managed only to grab the thin spaghetti-strap of my shoulder bag before a meaty hand snatched up my bony bicep and a gruff voice growled my name with exasperation, "*Coralie.*"

I sucked in a sharp breath before Paul swung me out of the danger zone of collapsing chunks of ceiling.

We stumbled forward, his hand slipping away from my arm. The crash of wood smacked down behind us with enough impact to cause a tremor of its own.

Distantly, I was aware of the shop door being booted open. The bell above it rang for a beat before it was drowned out by the sudden rise of crashes and

bangs and rattles ripping through the air. Sounded almost like a fast train tearing off the rails, if that heart-stopping noise was magnified to flood an entire town.

Footsteps pounded on the linoleum, piling ahead to the open glass door. We poured out onto the street, bodies slamming into bodies, arms bouncing off arms. A bag whacked me over the shoulder at one point, but I hardly felt it. I don't think I even noticed it at the time.

There was a moment out the front of the rattling shop; a moment of deafening songs of tremors, strangled breaths and shuddering bodies, and the flickers of torches giving off their faint light in the suffocating darkness.

The light did little. The dust in the air was too thick to see through—and I could already feel it starting to crawl down my itchy throat. Panicked gasps were breaking out all around me; everyone, suffocating on the dust spraying down from the buildings around us, hidden deep in the dark.

"Get to the middle of the road," a familiar gravelly voice commanded, and I recognised it even in the faint wispy light of the torches to belong to Paul. If we had a leader among us, it would be him. But in the cold, harsh reality, we are a band of individual survivors—each one of us out for themselves.

But an earthquake?

That was a danger we hadn't faced before. And sticking together was our best chance to survive.

We herded ourselves like sheep without a shepherd to the middle of the road. Before we could form a solid wall, someone squeezed into the middle of the group, and I caught the faint scent of peach-juice from a tin. It must have been Elsa, since she was devouring the canned peaches earlier before sleep came

for most of us.

I couldn't bring myself to be annoyed at Elsa for using us like shields against falling debris; wood house-faces and roof-tiles rolling down to crack against the cobblestone. Really, the tinge of annoyance that twisted my narrow face into a grimace was sprung through me purely because *I* hadn't thought of that.

A soft murmured voice somehow carried over the shattering violence in the air, "Shouldn't we find cover?"

That question speared memories through me.

Much of the year at Strath boarding school in Scotland meant a lot of days and nights spent binging TV shows. Drama, you know? And of course, earthquakes were a classic trope for those types of shows. So the memories came back to me in flashes, people seeking shelter in bathtubs with mattresses pulled over top, crammed underneath solid dining tables, hiding out anywhere but in the middle of the street—right between two danger points of collapsing buildings. But then, if they were collapsing, were they really all that safe?

"Stay tight," Paul grunted, the clutch of fear evident in his shaky undertones. His hand—sweaty and too-large—grips onto my shoulder firmly, and it was just in that moment that I realised we were all holding onto each other in a circle around Elsa. "Wait for the tremor to stop, then we run for it."

Run for it?

Run where?

Who knew how far this earthquake stretched? Did it reach other towns nearby, forgotten farms and lost villages?

All the ramblings and anxieties whirling around

my mind didn't bring an argument to my tongue. I had no better alternative. I wasn't the one with the plans around here. I was more of a follower—not because I wanted to be, but because I simply couldn't be bothered with the burden on my shoulders. The less weight to carry in this world, the better.

But now the weight of the world was raining down on us. Well the weight of Tours was, at least.

Beneath my feet, the shudders were starting to slow. Tremors were dying out. My breath hitched audibly and I dug my hold even tighter onto the stretched t-shirts I was gripping onto—Paul's and whoever else's. It was impossible to tell with the faint torches aimed down at the cobblestone.

I watched the stones.

Elsa was crouched over, hands pressed against the nape of her neck, shoulders hunched and head buried between her knees.

Bowed over her, we waited for the last shudders of the earthquake to dissolve, disappear back into the earth.

And when it did, we moved fast.

It might have come back. It very well should have since none of this could have been predicted, and the world is now just the opposite of that; it is wholly unpredictable.

The group jumped into shambles.

Hands snatched onto shoulders and fingers clutched the back of t-shirts and cardigans. The rapid thumps of our shoes smacked against the stones as we jogged in a line down the middle of the street. Unsteady, torchlight swerved over glimpses of debris and abandoned cars (whose roofs wore dents) and the glitter of pulverised glass on the ground.

Instinctively, we followed our plan and headed south. Well, *back* south. For months, we'd been moving around in circles, but it was time to circle around the dark fae when we could and find an already destroyed place by the coast. That was our plan. There, we might be able to rebuild some semblance of a life, with the sea to provide fish and nearby water to keep us alive.

So down the main road, we picked up the pace, sharp breaths and some gasping sounds starting to rise up from our single file. Bags slapped against backs, but mine just bounced against my hip. Lost my main backpack in the grocer's store, left behind. Now, all I had with me was my shoulder bag, too small to carry much of anything important. In it were some tampons, a pack of Marlboro cigarettes and a lighter, a small keychain torch, painkillers, a serrated kitchen-knife and a handgun that I've yet to use. But I'd lost everything else; clothes, washcloths, shoes, socks and underwear, books, a pack of kindling—*and food*. Tins and cans and packets, all crammed into that backpack, all gone.

There was no going back for it, either. Not without parting ways with the group, and I'm no fool. I stuck with them all the way down the sloped street, until it happened all at once—

The force of the tremor was enough to knock me off my feet. Like dolls cut from strings, we all went toppling over. Few still stayed standing.

As I smacked onto my side against the cobblestone—even with the quivering beneath me that rattled me like an explosion of shudders in my body—I couldn't tear my eyes off of it.

At the bottom of the cobblestone downhill road, amber light shone up in warped rivers. And my heart sank all the way to my watery gut at the sight of them—

at the sight of the dark fae army.

Let me take you back there, to the last time I *almost* died…

3
WHEN THE FAE CAME

The dark fae haven't spotted us yet.

Preoccupied by the violent tremors downhill at the cusp of the town, they focus all their attention on the earth. It's worse down there—even beasts like the dark fae wear unease in the thinning of their lips, the tilts of their mouths, the uncertain steps back that they take, as though fighting the urge to retreat—an urge I doubt comes naturally to these warriors.

Each time I lay my gaze upon these creatures, I'm stunned still and silent. Never before has anything in this world been so beautiful yet savage all at once. Not our lions, our tigers, even our storms.

These beings are something else entirely with their ghost-white faces, flawless as though they are sculpted marble; others with beige tones to compliment honey-brown eyes so deep that even from this distance, I think fleetingly of pools of fresh mud and riverbanks. I catch amber eyes, like the early kisses of flames that come from their fire-torches.

And I spot among the masses of them that they have captured a group of humans somewhere along their travels.

The humans are unmistakable in their decrepit appearances next to such creatures. They huddle together, clothes turned to rags that hang off their bony frames, faces hollowed out by hunger and terror, sunken in and illuminated by the hot orange fire-torches.

In contrast, despite the fae's obvious beauty, the

savagery of what they are shouts louder than the earthquake. It's in the almond-shapes of their blade-like eyes, the cruel pinches of their brows and mouths even while eyeing the dangerous earth with creases of worry, and the sheer size of them. They are towers next to a tall human man, that's for sure.

Most look around the mid-six-foots, but some stretch up even taller than that. But it's more than height; it's the pull of their leather armour over bulging muscles, the circumference of their biceps thicker than my thighs in some of them.

Each of them carries an abundance of weapons. *An American's dream*, I think bitterly to myself. Belts of knives and blades, swords sheathed at their backs, razored whips coiled around muscular forearms.

The terror at seeing them so close to us—so close to where we were resting not long before—has our whole group motionless. We have turned to statues, all flattened to the ground, hands spread out, heads down, eyes darting around.

One wrong move, and all attention of the dark fae could fix right uphill—on us. For the moment, they watch the tremors wrack the earth. But that could change with a too-loud breath or a shift of the body. We are mere heartbeats away from being discovered.

But then, for the first time in a long while, fate seems to look kindly on us—or at the very least, with pity.

The earth splits.

At the edge of the dark fae army, where hundreds of them are gathered, the most ground-wracking tremor strikes through the whole town. Dirt and tarmac are speared with a crack too fast, too sudden, too violent.

My heart leaps up into my throat as some of the

captive humans go tumbling into the widening crack. One has managed to grip into the earth at the edge, keeping herself up. But no one comes to her aid; not even her own kind. And it's a mere ragged breath loosened from my tight chest before she's falling into the opening pit.

Fleetingly, I wonder if there is lava down there, if it runs that deep into the earth, and the girl burned alive or melted. But the thought is hit right out of me when it happens; the crack is spearing uphill. It's headed right towards *us*.

I have barely a moment to see the dark fae spread out, backing off from the earthquake and the area, and that a handful of them are trapped on the other side of the crack. They separate, and the handful are riding what looks to be hairless horses adjacent to the crack, coming our way.

I launch myself up from the ground. And I go sprinting down the road.

Everyone else in the group has the same idea. No more single-file lines, organised movements. We sprint, as fast as we can, and I know someone is too slow when I hear a gurgling cry and the split of earth behind me.

I don't look back. I jump to the side just as a pile of roof-tiles comes smacking down on the road. Houses all around are crumbling to chunks and debris.

I dodge and duck and dive, avoiding it all. Somehow, Paul got ahead of me with Kale. Maybe I'm too slow, maybe they were ahead of me the whole time. I don't know. But I do hear the thumping of bootfalls behind me, right at my heels.

But then behind me, there's a sudden rise of mangled screams. And a very, very audible crunch.

I stagger, my heeled ankle boots skidding against the cobblestone. Stumbling around, my shoulder collides hard with Laura barging past me. She keeps going as I search the growing darkness for the victims I heard—obviously crushed by some debris.

I don't get another second to look or investigate before orange light rises up ahead and my heart stops. Those dark fae divided from their group are coming.

And they are close.

I turn on my heels and I bolt into the dark. I use only the sounds of footsteps pounding against the road to guide me, smacking into car doors and tripping over abandoned bags of rubbish.

We run for too long.

I don't know if we have left the town behind, or have come into another one when we finally slow. All I know is that we have lost some people, the earth doesn't shudder with the tremors anymore, and my legs are searing from the inside.

And one more thing...

Those stragglers—the dark fae separated from their army—are not far behind us.

4
AFTER THE FAE CAME

That dark fae army—in the hundreds—should have cornered and killed us.

They should have had their chance to do what they do; burn places to the ground, torture humans they find, *slaughter*.

If it wasn't for that earthquake, that saving grace, we would all be dead. Or worse (after seeing the proof of human prisoners in the army with my own eyes) we could have been captured.

France is my home. It always has been, since I never considered boarding school to be even a home away from home. So I know that earthquakes just don't happen here.

Whatever caused it has been the talk of the group since we holed up in this dirty, musty flat in the next village over (we figured out with street signs and our map that we ran all the way to Saint-Roch while fleeing the fae stragglers and the earthquake). Some of the others think that it was the earth rejecting the invasion—all the bloodshed, the darkness, the plague. But all that I can agree with in that reasoning is the perpetual blackness of the world. All the rest of it has been a reoccurrence throughout human history, so I don't see why Mother Earth would get all up in arms about some virus and wars. We've done worse, us humans.

Even the darkness is something we have done before, though clearly not to the same extent. But what we have done is covered our cities in smog, so thick that the sun couldn't penetrate.

So why would Mother Earth be on our side now?

I'm not buying into the theories flying about this crammed 'kitchen' … if you could call it that.

Maybe, since my life before the dark was all finer things and wealth and villas on the beachside towns and trips to the Swiss Alps, I'm a little on the judgey side, but this … *kitchen* reminds me of those found in the budget holiday vehicles; caravans. Mind, I've only ever seen the interior of those things on TV, but still. That's what this kitchen reminds me of with its boxed-in space, crammed full to the brim with our remaining survivors, a hob instead of a full oven-cooker, no air-fryer in sight, a dirty white kettle that will never boil no matter how much I pray to Mother Earth that it will.

It's made fuller by the couch and armchair we pushed in here not long after we settled in. I've found a cosy spot on the corner of the couch, leaning against the thick arm whose material stinks of stale cigarettes and spilled beer.

It brings an idea to mind. I rummage through my shoulder bag and pluck out a French cigarette and lighter. No one bothers to even glare at me. Not like I can go outside for a smoke, can I? Besides, this is still France. And some of the others are too deep in sleep to notice.

While some of the others sleep, most of us are wallowing in the silence that swallowed us a little while ago. Paul went back to scout the road leading into the village. We need to know if those straggler fae are coming our way. And he still hasn't returned. Each second that door doesn't open and he doesn't step inside, is another second my breath feels too tight in my chest.

But the silence is more than impatience. It's sorrowful, too. Respectful, on my part.

We lost three between the earthquake and the flat.

The quiet lone-wolf of the group, Adler, somehow vanished. He must have gotten separated from us while we ran out of the town, forever gone to the dark now. Maybe he's still out there, wandering, searching for us. Or—more likely—the tough German will do just fine on his own.

The others we lost (two of them), I heard being crushed by debris. I've since learned that those two were Nate and Miranda—two British siblings, no older than me in my final year at boarding school. At least I had the chance to leave for university, but those two only had the opportunity of a world strangled by darkness and war.

Our numbers are down to eight now. Less if Paul doesn't return. The stubborn bull insisted on going it alone. 'Can't risk more people', he gruffed when Laura offered to go with him.

Laura is as close to bravery as we have among the girls here. She's a close second to Paul. The rest of us don't do so well in the courage-department.

I tried to be friends with her once (partly for protection, I won't lie), but I've never been skilled at things like that and now she thinks I'm a 'pretentious twat'. Her words, not mine. Said them right to my face. Apparently, she values herself higher than me because she knows how to hunt and live off the land, but I don't.

Even in this whole new world, I guess these things still matter to some.

Not to me, it doesn't. All that matters now is

survival.

But even now, we know that survival has gone from a hope to a fantasy.

Paul bursts into my thoughts when he comes barging through the kitchen door. The sudden sound yanks everyone out of their stupor. The ones who were asleep jerk forward, eyes wide and panicked, hands reaching for nearby weapons.

My slim cigarette hovers near my parted, chapped lips, vapours of smoke slithering out of me; anticipation freezes me.

When gazes land on Paul as he shuts the door quietly then leans back on it, a ribbon of relief unwinds over us, and we all go back to poor posture, slumped.

He's alive. He wasn't followed.

For a minute, we're safe.

I take a breath of my cigarette, hearing the paper crackle in the quiet.

Still, eyes follow Paul as he slides down the door and rests his forearms on his drawn-up knees. His gaze darts around the kitchen for a beat before he shakes his head.

My face falls. Blood rains out of my head and piles around my thumping heart. My hand lowers, lingering the cigarette between my knees, ribbons of smoke lifting up from it as it turns to ash.

"They are coming this way," he tells us. "Four of them." As an afterthought, he adds, "Saw no signs of the army."

His add-on has no effect on the utter defeat deflating me. Four dark fae are more than enough to take us all out. Just one of them could do more damage than that. I've seen these things in battle—I've seen them rip out throats with their teeth and plunge their hands into ribcages. Gruesome stuff; the kind that sticks to dreams and turns them ghastly.

Paul leans his head back against the door. Looking up at the popcorn ceiling, he says, "I assume they are going around to meet back up with their army. They know where they are and how to find them. So even if we move on before they get here…"

He trails off and the implications hang heavy over us. My head bows as I bring up my knees to my chest. My white country-dress slips back as I rest my chin on my knees. My cigarette hand rests over the arm of the couch, going unsmoked. A long line of ash falls to the linoleum floor.

Either way, we are stuck in the middle of dark fae—and who knows however many other armies are out there in the black. This village hasn't been touched yet, and that means that some fae armies haven't finished what they started—so there should be more coming.

Surrounded, I see no way out of this. And apparently, neither does anyone else.

I mean, it could be the world wearing us down to scraps. We've been at this a long time. Over a year. I don't know exactly how long, but it's been time that has stretched us from hopeful to absolutely desolate and hopeless.

I can't stop the thought from invading my mind—what if none of us really want to keep at it anymore? We have no more fleeing, running, escaping left in us.

And our fantasies of life by the sea are just that— fantasies. How can we adapt to a proper life in the dark? Who's to say that we won't be found by other armies—or even other survivors, the none-too-kind ones that aren't exactly rare.

None of us offer up any solutions. Well, not until Harry speaks up—

"We could fight." His voice is small, broken by how unused it is. He's not much of a chatterbox.

All gazes cut to him.

Silence sweeps over us, an expectant and laughable tint to it.

With a bitter smile, I finish off my cigarette then flick it to the floor. Using the toe of my boot, I stamp it out, then bring up my knee to my chest again.

Paul is the one who answers, "Fight against the dark fae?" He manages to fight off the incredulity from his tone, though I recognise it in the corner creases of his eyes.

"*We*," Harry repeats, elbowing his only friend in the group, Jamie, "could fight."

I lift my chin from my knees and narrow my eyes on them. Confusion is etched onto the grim tilt of my mouth.

Jamie shoots his friend a baffled look.

"We have everything we need in this room," Harry goes on, his mind churning behind his bottle-green eyes, working faster than he can speak.

"We wouldn't stand a chance," Spike—he *says* that's his name, but I doubt it to this day—argues, an irritated edge to his tone. "They'd massacre us all before we could lift a knife!"

"No, no, we wouldn't have to get close, not at first," Harry says, his eyes lighting up. "We build *a bomb*. That gives us a chance to …"

"Finish them off," I say, eyeing him with a whole new outlook. Smart cookie. Bet he was destined to be some genius before all this shit happened.

He looks the part, too. Pimples—all red, angry and yellow-tipped—litter his chin and cheeks, and his auburn hair wears the oil carried from weeks of not washing it. Beneath his baggy, torn t-shirt (with some cartoon character on the front, go figure) he is all scrawny skin-and-bones.

But if the kid says he knows how to build a bomb, then good for him. And it might make the difference between going out with a blast and going out with a sizzle.

I'm leaning towards the blast idea.

I'm the first to nod.

Paul watches me for a long, quiet moment. Then he nods, too.

It's a ripple after that. All except Spike seem to agree, even if none of us are terribly happy about it.

Finally, Spike pushes up from the cabinet beneath the stained sink and strides to the pantry. He rummages through it for a moment before he pulls back, holding two bottles in his hands; cheap whiskeys caked in dust.

"Well if this is it, then I want to have to some fun." He grins something oily, baring his plaque-stained teeth at us. I suppress a shudder. "Who's with me?"

Only Laura reaches out her hand for a bottle.

I roll onto my side and lay there. I stare at the wall.

And silently, I listen as the next few hours roll on. There's the clinking of glass, the glugging of whiskey, and the two weeds in the corner, working on the bomb.

Snares of sleep dare start to wrap around me.

I don't know how long I've been tucked up here, but just when the murmurs in the kitchen begin to muffle, my eyelids are fluttering and my mind has drifted off to that strange place between sleep and reality.

In a life full of almosts, slumber only threatens to take me. It starts to. But before it can secure its grip on my melting mind, I hear it—a heavy skittering sound.

I blink, awake.

Looking at the wall, a frown knits my blonde eyebrows together and I listen. Maybe I just imagined it. It could have been a sound of my strange dreamlike thoughts.

Then it skitters out again, this time followed by a wet slapping sound, like a pile of squids being dropped to the floor, then rolling down wooden stairs.

The unusual blend of noise has disturbed the whole group. The rustle of jackets and bags being moved crawls through the room. Then a hush rolls over us.

Whatever that alien sound is, it's coming from outside. And my churning, watery gut is telling me it isn't good.

5
NOW

Paul is the first to move, but Spike—fuelled by liquid courage—suddenly decides to take charge. He pushes up from the wall, staggers a step before he rights himself.

Eyes are glued to him as he strides to the window, hidden by sheet-metal blinds. He carries a grotesque swagger with him all the way. Loose in his hand, swinging at his side, is a thin torch that I can tell just by looking at, its light won't be strong enough to see down the three stories to the street below.

Still, he is undeterred, and he pauses by the window before craning his neck to glare at us all and push his bony finger against his lips. Something inside of me prickles and I have the urge to put laxatives in his whiskey.

With a flick of his thumb, the faint white light wisps out of the torch and illuminates the dust particles clinging to the air. He lifts the torch as he peels down a slat of metal and peers out into the thick black.

My breath is trapped in my chest.

He aims the light outside and—

The glass blasts inwards. The window explodes into shattered pieces and Spike is thrown across the room from the sheer force of it.

The window is suddenly pulverised specks shredding through the kitchen. I have just enough time to throw myself over the arm of the couch. The couch is a shield against the violent rainfall of glass and I land beside Paul.

He has flattened himself to the ground, hands folded over his head. At his feet is where Spike landed, and he's all crumpled up like a crushed sheet of paper.

Skt skt skt, skrrrrrtttt.

That strange skittering sound is suddenly screaming above me, so loud that I cringe against the linoleum floor and slap my hands to my ears. Whatever is making that noise, it has smashed inside through the window and now it's in here *with* us.

Sllllrrrrpppp, sllrrpp, sllllrrrrpppp.

Torches are ignited all around the kitchen. The dotted light is barely enough to pierce the thick darkness rolling in through the window.

I'm about to push up from the floor and make for the door when I hear it; over the sickening slapping, skittering noises above, a scream splits the air.

I throw a wild glare around the room, keeping myself low enough to avoid the growing, swelling dark cloud above (and whatever the fuck is inside that cloud). My gaze passes over the knocked-out Spike, who is being shaken awake by Paul, before it lands on the man screaming.

It's Jamie—one of the weeds working on the bomb.

Something …

*Some…**thing*** has uncoiled from the black cloud and wrapped around his scrawny bicep. It … it looks like some sort of black, razored tentacle dripping with a clear slime.

Flashes of the film *Alien* invades my mind and I instantly recoil.

The razored edge of the tentacle pierces into Jamie's arm deep enough that a pool of blood is swelling on the floor, and each time he jerks against it, his scream twists with searing agony.

He's lost it, now. He's writhing, kicking, screaming out for help. It's Harry who jolts up first, and he grabs his looted samurai sword as he rises up.

Winks of the silver blade catch in the light before he brings down the sword and cuts the tentacle from the cloud. A strangled hiss shudders through the cloud. And it writhes as though it's alive.

It's all I need to hear and see before I'm shoving to my feet. I barge into the kitchen door, crouched low to avoid the fog, and fumble with the door handle.

By the time I've wrestled the door open, a crowd of us has gathered, and we're all scrambling out of there.

I don't know who's behind me. I just bolt through the flat, my boots smacking on carpet, and I barrel into the hallway. Rushed footsteps follow me all the way down to the main floor, but I pause before I head for the front door—the same door that leads out onto the street, where those tentacle things came from.

A sweaty hand snatches up my wrist. I swing a glare over my shoulder and I see Spike. He looks as pale as the whites of his eyes, the terror of what just happened betrayed in the tremor clinging to him.

"Back," he manages to wheeze.

Paul rushes up behind him—he must have stuck around in the kitchen, waiting for everyone to get out before he fled. His breathing is hard and rough when he says, "There's a back exit. This way—"

He turns and runs through the lobby to a narrow metal door. The group regathers for a moment before we all rush after Paul. I don't get a second to look at the faces around me, to see who made it, or if Jamie was killed by whatever that thing was.

The front door to the complex is blasted open.

In a heartbeat, the skittering and slapping sound of those tentacle critters invades the space, and we're all racing through the backdoor to safety.

The sound of the backdoor slamming shut vibrates through the narrow corridor we pile into, but I don't pay it any mind—I spear through the hall, sticking close to the heels of Laura in front of me. Her brown hair whips back, smacking me across the face, when she does a double take.

I take the opportunity and barrel around her. Now, I'm caught up to Paul—and just in time.

The critters have reached us. The backdoor rattles just as Paul shoulders the last of the doors, the one leading out into the lane behind the complex. It caves in on the last hit, and we go piling out into the dark.

Instinctively, I snatch onto the hem of Paul's t-shirt. Someone grabs onto the back of my dress, and it's a domino effect. Those of us who survived to make it out to the lane are grabbing onto each other, single-file, and we take off running blind.

I can only assume Paul is doing the same as me—free arm spread out, feeling for any walls we might slam into. But we make good work of sticking to the middle of the lane. We don't slow down as we follow the curve onto another road, then cut back to the start of the village.

No one dares turn on a torch. Last time we did, those critters came crashing through the flat window, and did god-knows-what to Jamie.

Jamie. I wonder if he's still alive. I wonder if Harry grabbed the bomb they were working on before he got the hell out of there. Or is he lost behind in the flat with those critters from the pits of the darkness?

No time to waste on thoughts of others. The skittering sound, clicking and clacking, is at our heels, gaining closer.

My outstretched hand smacks into something solid and I suck in a sharp breath. My heart skips a beat as I recoil.

Paul felt it, too. He stops suddenly and, one-by-one, we all smack into each other. I get the worst of it, my forehead cracking right off the back of Paul's skull.

Wincing, I fight the instinct to touch the sudden ache springing on my head, and feel out my free hand through the darkness. Each clacking sound grows louder with the picked-up pace of my thrumming heart.

It's a car, I realise.

Paul confirms this when he shouts, his booming voice breaking the suffocating darkness, "Take cover!"

So we do.

I might be the first to move or the last. In the dark, it's impossible to tell. All I know for sure is something happens to my hearing—I can listen only to a high-pitched ringing sound, not the scramble of people—as I drop to the cobblestone, then roll myself under the abandoned car.

The skittering passes overhead.

The clacking and slapping skulks right by me, so close that I have to press my sweaty palms to my face to stifle my breath. One noise too loud and I could be a goner.

I just shut my eyes on the gloom, listen to the ringing in my ears, the critters sweeping past me, and feel the pulse of my blood swelling throughout my body.

Curling my body up into a ball, I squeeze my eyes

shut tighter and slowly, start to hear the others over the ringing. A scream that sounds so far away that it could belong to a street on the other side of the village; a struggle, boots and hands smacking against the ground, a hard grunt. Then … silence.

Critters got one of us.

I don't know who. I don't care, as long as it isn't me.

*

A part of me distantly wonders if it's better to be killed by the dark fae than these strange new critters, born of darkness.

Time passes, and we stay hidden all over the street. Not all of us could fit under the abandoned cars. I can only picture some of the group tucked up in doorways, hands over heads and sprawled out over the road, maybe some ran off.

But finally, the critters leave, taking their sickening sounds with them. They roll off into the distance, in search of new victims.

Fleetingly, I let myself ask, 'Did the dark fae bring these things into this world to finish us off—the surviving stragglers?'

Not that it matters. If Harry survived and grabbed the bomb, we're all dead soon anyway. And if he didn't, it won't be much longer before we die. It's an unescapable fate that awaits us all. For me, I would just rather it be on my own terms. And deep down I hope I won't coward out at the last minute.

We wait a while of silence before the first of us moves. It isn't Paul, who's tucked up at my feet. It's someone across the street, if my hearing can be trusted—and it's a pretty well-honed skill after so long in the dark without sight.

It only takes one of us to start moving before we're all creeping out of our hiding spots. The sounds of boots and sneakers scrape over cobblestone, and I'm very aware of how quiet the noise is compared to usual. We have definitely lost some more people.

No one lights a torch—for good reason—and so I don't see who we lost. We all feel our way back to the middle of the street to regroup before someone leads the way to the nearest door.

Like the last one, this door leads to a complex of flats. We take the one on the top floor, but we don't break in the door. We loot keys from the front desk to ensure our silence. It's an unspoken agreement between us. Unspoken is the keyword here—no one speaks a word all the way into the flat.

In silence, we avoid the kitchen that overlooks the main street and hole up in the lounge instead. Paul breaks the quiet for the first time when he mutters that he will take first watch.

Before he goes to the kitchen to sit alone, he switches on his faint torch and hands it off to me.

I arch a brow as he adds in a low voice, "You can take over watch in a couple of hours."

A frown pinches between my brows and, just as I'm about to ask why me, I trace the aim of the torchlight to the musty couch against the wall—and I see the extent of what has happened to our group.

I understand, and Paul leaves for the kitchen.

Standing by the armchair, I look around the tattered group, turning the torch on each one of them. My light grows stronger as one by one, more start to flicker on. Our sense of safety is rising, or we are just too exhausted to care now that we have a moment to recover. Besides, we need the light if we're to take care of anyone's wounds.

And there are wounds aplenty.

My gaze lands on the floor, where a beige-tinted rug is starting to turn red. Jamie is sprawled out over it, somehow still with us. But with Harry and Mikey—a middle-aged Spanish man—crouched over him, I suppose he was carried out of danger and protected all the way here.

Jamie doesn't look so hot. His eyes are rolling to the back of his head, short lashes fluttering, and there's a build-up of white foam crawling out the corner of his mouth. But that's not what catches my whole attention—it's his arm, where the razored tentacles had coiled.

The flesh there has *blackened*. Looks rotten to the bone, about ready to fall off. And black lines—like wisps of dark clouds—are stretching up his bare shoulder.

I watch as Harry peels apart the tattered remains of Jamie's shirt. With his narrow torso revealed, it's all the easier to see the shaky rise and fall of his chest. His breathing is choppy and strained, and now that I listen over the shuffle of the room, I hear the hoarseness of it.

For a while, I just stand there, looking around the wounded. Someone has a deep gash running down the backside of his leg, from mid-thigh all the way down to his heel. At some point, I hear mutters that tell me he cut himself scrambling to get under a van.

The Spanish sisters, Silvia and Maria, aren't together anymore. Maria is nowhere to be seen, so I know she didn't make it back with us. She either perished out there or somehow lost us in the dark. Silvia is huddled up in the corner, nursing her knee. At first glance, I don't think much of her wound, but then Laura forces her hand back and reveals the truth of her injury—black lines, threading through her skin.

Tentacle critters got her too.

Our uninjured come to the rescue of the wounded. Not me. I stand too long in the middle of the room, unsure of myself. Spike is the only other one not to help, and I loathe that we have that in common. I loathe it so deeply to the bone that it spurs me into action. I don't help bind cuts—blood and torn flesh make me ill. Instead I trade the torch for a blanket then roll it over the curtain rod, blacking out the window.

Once that slight chore is done, I check what we normally do when we hole up in a new place: Find a bathroom, check the water works (it does), and refill some bottles, loot for batteries and medical supplies. When that's finished, I carry my small supply of paracetamol and two batteries to the lounge.

It's then that I learn Jamie didn't make it. Not like I expected otherwise, really.

Looks like it was the black lines that killed him. Now, the lines have reached his chest, curled as though they are poisonous lashes wound around his heart.

Harry is weeping beside him. He sniffs and uses the back of his hand to wipe away snot. Mikey drapes a blanket over the corpse. We'll have to keep him in here for a little while. Can't go dumping his body out in the hall or another flat just yet, not with the critters likely still nearby, and other survivors barely clinging onto the threads of life.

We respect the dead as much as we can in this dark world; this dark, cold world with a brand-new threat to wipe us all out.

It's never been clearer. We have to face off with these lone warriors headed our way. For me, it's about more than what awaits us if we don't put up a final fight—a part of me just wants this to be over. And that part is growing, swelling into an unavoidable abyss.

I need to fill it.

I need this all to be over.

I need to die—on my own terms.

6

Though there is no night and day anymore, no moon or sun to tell the time, the adrenaline of the day has now simmered through the group and softened us into a faint state of exhaustion, leaving me to *feel* like it's night.

Parked on the table pushed up against the back wall, I drift my attention around the room. Most of the others have been lured by sleep—they are curled up around the not-working heater, tucked close together on the couch, sleeping wherever they can. Can't blame them. Even my eyelids are starting to gain weight, growing heavier by the minute.

I blink the weariness away and glance over at Harry. Alone, he works on the homemade bomb that he managed to salvage when the critters first attacked us. Clearly, he does it to distract himself, or feel betterresigned to the fate of his friend. I don't know why, but I'm just glad he keeps tinkering away on it. We need it up and running soon.

You know, before now, the sight of a homemade bomb would have terrified me, speared white-cold fear right through me. Especially when the terrorism-fear was climbing the walls to the skies. Now, it's almost a welcome reprieve from all that we suffer.

Harry pauses his work for a moment. I watch as he slowly—reluctance clinging to his stiff muscles— glances over his shoulder at the hidden bodies. His eyes are bloodshot red, and at the blushed bottom of his nose, scabs have started to appear on the skin.

He shakes his head before he turns back to his work.

His friend's corpse is still under the stiff, itchy blanket. *Jamie* (Don't forget their names. Try to remember them all). Name or no name, he's now joined by Silvia, and her swift death confirmed that there's something toxic about those razored tentacles— something that, no matter where they get you, makes certain you die.

It's a strange thing to realise, isn't it? That everything in your life you have done up to this point— trapped in the thick blackness with monsters—was all for nothing.

Harry can't say the same about himself. Whatever he has done in his life (excelled at chemistry, maybe?) has come to this point, where he is our best weapon in our final stand.

But me?

What have I done that has led to this moment, that has somehow benefited me and the group, helped me survive?

I'm not afraid of death, so there's that. I've tried to dip my toes in the other side before with bottles of pills and vodka. Unsuccessfully, of course.

But what can I confess to have done that has made a difference somehow?

Nothing. I'm useless to this group, in this new world, and I know it too. Maybe the others know it— they see me for the fraud I am, the once-pampered 'princess' with wealth and connections to a world long lost.

None of that matters anymore. I'd say what's kept me alive so far is my complete ambivalence to life. That, and the languages I have under my belt. I can communicate with most of those in the group, since I'm fluent in English, French and Spanish. I know a little Italian—and that skill alone earned me a free tin of mac and cheese a few months back.

The memory of that cold, gloopy pasta floods my mouth with saliva. Deep in my belly, growls start to rise up. I press my hand to my tummy and press tight.

Lost all my food back in the grocer's shop when the earthquake hit. I've got nothing. Just to be sure, I swing my shoulder bag around to rest on my lap. It's fairly small, so everything I've crammed in there needs to be removed piece by piece—no space for rummaging around.

I keep the handgun out, since I'll be on watch soon.

And as I expected, nothing to eat can be found in my bag. No chocolate bars, lone sweets, or even crumbs.

I pack everything back into it carefully (though I do light a slim cigarette) then slump back against the wall.

Just as I get comfortable, a flicker of movement catches my focus and I look over at the door. Spike has pushed up from the floor where he was resting, and he's wandering over to me.

I almost snarl him away, but then I spot what's clenched in his right fist. A nougat bar, coated in chocolate. A type that's tough to get on this side of France.

I watch him as I exhale a cloud of smoke.

For some reason, he sits on the table so close to me that our hips are almost touching, then he decides to do the classic man-spread, stretching out his thighs and pushing way too far into my personal space.

My eyes roll back before I scoot away a bit. Normally, I would have man-spreaded right back at him. But since we're all about to die very soon—and he has a nougat bar for me—I don't much see the point. But I am careful to flick some ash onto his leg. He doesn't notice.

He hands me the snack.

I don't bother with a thanks before I tear off the plastic wrapper, then let it flitter to the floor.

I stamp out my cigarette on the table.

"Do we even know where they are anymore?" Spike asks after a while. He scratches the pimpled-stubble on his pointy chin.

I shoot him a perplexed look, mouth full of nougat, my faintly freckled cheeks bulging. My voice is muffled by chocolate as I ask, "E-r hoo iv?"

Somehow, he still seems to understand me. "The dark fae, the ones separated from their group. We've been pushed out of their path, maybe pushed towards the rest of their army."

I shrug, my mind answering where my full mouth cannot, *'Then we will take on the army.'*

Death will come much swifter that way.

But though it is unspoken, it's obvious what our next move will be. It's the only way to do it: When we're certain it's clear, and the lone warriors have had enough time to catch up with us, we'll double back to the main street.

First, we need to make sure the bomb is ready. Without it, there will be little purpose to what we're planning on doing other than simply walking into our deaths. If that's all we wanted to do, we would form a suicide pact here in the flat and just shoot each other.

No, it's more than just a craving for the finale, a longing to end the suffering and tedium. It's the vindictive victory in taking a few of them out with us.

Bringing them down as far as we can.

Who knows, maybe by taking out these few warriors, we might be saving other lives out there? If there are many left to save, that is. Which I doubt.

Earlier days saw more survivors. Now, starvation, infection, the dark and its dangers, wild animals—it all has led to a complete dwindle of our numbers. The dark fae really are here to wipe us out completely—an extinction.

But then, that doesn't explain what I saw in the army; the group of humans with them. Their prisoners.

"Did you see them?" I ask Spike once I've finished off the bar. I suck chocolate and nougat residue from my teeth. "The curries or whatever you called them."

"Koo-rees," he corrects me, his voice muffled by past pains. He looks down at his hands threaded together between his spread legs. "Kuris. Yeah, I saw them."

Spike has had a lot to say about these 'kuris'. Before I spotted the human prisoners in the army, I must admit, I didn't believe his stories. Most of us just brushed him off.

Before we came across him a couple of months ago, he claimed to have been kidnapped by a band of dark fae. A smaller army, but one packed with warriors all the same. They had slaughtered his fellow survivors before they searched his body—apparently stripped him clean—and found a crooked line of three freckles on his back. That, he said, is what saved him. The freckles.

I can't say why or even pretend to know, but those freckles apparently mean something to the dark fae. And it's what spared Spike's life. He was taken into the army to join the group of twenty-odd other humans (all with the same markings somewhere on their bodies) and they were forced into … well, slave labour.

According to Spike, they were called the 'kuris' by the dark fae, and they were made to wash their armour and cook their food and pitch their tents and start their fires.

He doesn't go into his time with the dark fae army any more than that. And before I saw a group of humans with the dark fae, I didn't believe him at all. I didn't believe that they would keep humans alive because of some freckles, and I certainly didn't believe that he managed to escape when another human survivor group started shooting at their camp one night.

As it went, turns out he wasn't lying. At least not about everything. Now I know for certain, they do keep humans with them—likely for slavery for their journey. What freckles have to do with it beyond meaning the difference between life and death, I can't even guess.

"Let me see them," I say and rub my hands clean of chocolate stains. "Your freckles."

He shifts around and, craning his arm back, lifts his blue t-shirt. The three freckles are crooked, I notice. They dot down his spine, the last one curving off-line. Reminds me somewhat of the stars in the lost-sky, Orion's Belt. Those were always my favourite stars back in the day—those and Sirius, of course.

He drops his top. It falls back into place, crumpled at the waistline of his blue jeans, and he shifts back around, angled towards me.

He tells me, "If this all fails—" he throws his hand around the room, gesturing to us, gesturing to the plan "—then I'll show them my freckles."

I arch a blonde, microbladed brow (I've had

some dermal fillers too, but that wears off eventually).
"You think it will save your life a second time?"

"Can't hurt," he says with a shrug. Then he turns his gaze up at me, his head bowed, and there's something sheepish in the way he regards me. "You could show yours too."

I blink, stunned. "What?"

"Your freckles. They might save you, too."

A frown pinches between my brow.

At first, I think of the faint dusting of freckles on my cheeks and nose; but none of those are in a crooked line—they are barely even three shades darker than my complexion. It's as though I'm permanently wearing an off-brand concealer.

Then, it hits me like a punch to the gut. I feel sick—and I know what freckles he's talking about.

Slowly, hot bubbles of anger start to rise up in my chest until rage is boiling over around my beating heart.

The urge to punch him straight off this table seizes me so strongly that I clench my fist. Prickles roll over my skin like ice-cold water, and my shoulders stiffen so hard that they quickly start to ache.

Through clenched teeth, I hiss, "I never told you about those." I roll my jaw then suck in a long, deep breath before I slit my eyes at him. "How do you know, Spike?"

How *does* he know about the three crooked-line freckles on the side of my right breast? How could he possibly know about those—unless…

And that hatred I have for him rises back up like a tornado.

Before I can boot out at him or swing or lunge, he holds up his hands in surrender, as though sensing the violence swirling around me.

"Look, it was an accident. I didn't know you were in the bedroom—it was a few towns back, and you were changing clothes, and I came to the door and it was cracked open a bit. I looked inside, but I didn't think I would see you in your knickers, all right?"

I don't believe him.

And I definitely don't get changed or undressed with the door open, even ajar.

I cave to the urges and lean back. My boot comes flying out at him before he even has a moment to blink. I catch him straight in the gut.

He doubles over. I slip off the table, grab my handgun and my bag, then storm out of the lounge, through the kitchen door.

7

Paul is sitting at the window, perched on the sill that's far too narrow for his bulky frame. He looks up from his pocketbook (the ones with black-leather covers, but no titles, since they have been worn-off over time) as I come in.

He reads my scowl all too easily. "What's he done now?" Exasperation clings to his tone and he softly folds his book closed.

"Spying on me while I change clothes," I growl and stomp over to him. My hands are balled at my sides. "Says it was an accident."

"It always is with him," Paul mutters and shakes his head. "He won't be a problem much longer," he adds as if to reassure me, comfort me somehow with the truth that we will all be dead shortly.

"I hope he dies most painfully of all of us."

Paul's mouth pulls into a tight line. He doesn't speak as he shifts off the window sill.

"You two just need to stay away from each other," he adds after a pause, and he pockets the book in his jeans. "After last time—"

"Oh, I hit him again," I confess without the slightest hint of regret or shame to cloud me. I merely blink, unperturbed. "He deserved it then and he deserves it now."

You see, Spike and I have a bit of a history. Let's just say I don't like the way he speaks to the girls around here. He's the kind who claims to be a 'nice guy', and it's a rule of thumb that when a guy self-professes himself that way, he's in fact the exact opposite.

I don't make the rules.

Besides, one day—after rejecting him by a lake we stopped to make camp at—he hit on me. The usual. Asked if we should "bunk" together that night.

To no surprise of mine, when I said no, he called me a "rich bitch" and "frigid". I showed him how much of a bitch I can be. I stomped on his toes so hard that he had a limp for a week, and his foot was all bruised and swollen.

Fingers crossed I actually did some real damage.

"I'll take over," I say with a sigh.

Paul nods and I can tell that my timing couldn't have been better for him. His eyelids are fighting him, drooping over his glass-blue eyes so unlike my ocean-blue ones, and he stretches his arms over his head.

He rolls his shoulders. I hear a faint clicking sound that brings a shudder through me—much too close to the noises of the critters.

Thinking of which...

"Have you heard them?" I ask.

He shakes his head. "It's clear out there. I'll use the bathroom," he adds, "before I head out to scout for those lone ones."

The lone ones. The separated dark fae warriors.

My stomach turns cold at the reminder. It's starting to feel real, less like a fantasy and plan, more like a looming reality.

I nod and wander past him to the window. I hop up on the sill. I'm narrow enough to fit on it comfortably.

The swing of the kitchen door tells me that Paul has left. Turning the gun over in my slender hands, I study the curtains that shield the window. Best not to slide them open just yet. Wait for Paul to scout first before I start to feel too safe.

But I know what's out there by the style of this flat. We've been in many like it before. No fire escape, just a straight-down fall to the cobblestone below. The main road must be close by.

A part of me flutters at the idea of a fire escape. There was one outside my room back at boarding school. I used to sit out there in the middle of the night and sneak a joint. Helped relax me for bed. Or I just wanted to numb myself. Whatever reason I indulged in it, I was only ever caught once and it wasn't at school. It was a maid at our villa, on my bedroom balcony, and of course she told my parents. But they never brought it up with me.

They never cared about much that I did. Even when I OD'd on painkillers and sleeping pills. Our family was the type to keep things quiet.

Hush, hush—our unofficial motto.

I could have snorted a line of coke in front of my parents and I swear they would have just turned their heads. That's if they would have even noticed.

If they did notice, the worst they would have done would have been to send me back to boarding school over the holidays. It was rare for me to be allowed to return home for the holidays, even Christmas. My last December at school, my parents left me there so that they could go to the Swiss Alps and all the charity events without me.

It wasn't a lonely Christmas, though. Most of the kids at the school were left behind. We just did Secret Santa, and that was enough for most of us. That year, my secret present-giver gifted me diamond earrings. Never wore them. Not much of a jewellery person.

Never much thought they looked all that good or saw the point of them. Mother's favourite pearls, I think, looked wretched and out-dated.

No pearls or diamonds in my life anymore.

I wonder if my parents died from the plague after I was taken by it. Maybe they went to a different sanatorium than the one they sent me to?

Then, a strange thought strikes me.

Did I survive the plague—just like Spike and all those human prisoners—because of the freckles?

Of course not. That's a silly thought and I chide myself for it, shaking my head. There are plenty in the group who don't have those freckles and who did suffer and survive the plague.

I'm putting too much weight on Spike and his theories. Who knows if the freckles have anything to do with why the dark fae spare some humans along the way?

My mind spirals too quickly into nonsense. That's what my House Teacher told me, at least.

With a sigh, I sink back against the window curve and watch the crimson curtains as though they themselves are the darkness beyond them. Silence is all that greets me. Silence is good. Means there are no dark fae armies descending upon the village, or any of those creatures lurking in the black.

The quiet has had a change on me in these bleaker times. It doesn't lull me to sleep like it used to. Now, it keeps me alert, because it means that the rest of the group are likely asleep and someone has to keep an ear and eye out for anything that might come our way.

Too many dangers out there to let myself relax with all the others. And the critters are just another threat to be worried about.

I stay on 'watch'—as close to watch as I can get without peeking through the curtains.

I ache to fidget, to do something other than just sit here listening to nothing. So I fiddle with my gun. I'm not too familiar with it. Never fired it before. But I know how, thanks to Paul.

I check that the safety switch is flicked on, then count the bullets in the clip. Fully loaded. I have another clip in my shoulder bag, but it's only got four bullets in it.

We'll face dark fae stragglers soon. I plan on shooting at them if they survive the bomb just to secure the promise of a swift death. They'll be furious and quick about it; likely slice off my head before I can feel anything. Anne-Boleyn-Style.

The fight is in my bones. I'm prepared, but more than that, I'm ready. I'm almost relieved beneath the icy fear. It's a formidable thing what we are going to do, but there's a sweet mercy in it, too.

Still, the nerves biting at me keep me awake for a long time. I tuck my gun into my brown suede ankle-boot, deep enough that it's secure yet definitely not in line with gun-safety rules.

Not that I give a damn.

I don't give a damn about much anymore.

*

After hours of staring at the curtain, the door swings open. I toss a glance over to it, seeing Laura slip into the kitchen.

"Bathroom is free," she tells me, and it lets me know more than just that people have been taking turns washing up. It lets me know that people *can* queue to wash up, which means all of our injured and wounded have died. They need no more care.

Who died?

I want to ask, but I decide against my morbid curiosity. Glad I wasn't in there to witness it all. I have a weak stomach. Too weak for this world.

Laura has her serrated hunting knife out of its holster; it's firm in her grip as she wanders over to me, and I know she's ready to take over watch.

I slip off the sill. "Paul back yet?"

She nods. "Got back about twenty minutes ago. The stragglers are on the main road," she tells me. "He saw them because they had torchlight with them—" not the torches we use of course, but those old-fashioned sticks with real fire at the end. "—and they were reading a map, trying to get their bearings. We're heading to the end of the village to cut them off in about an hour."

I nod, my heart sinking all the way down to my watery gut. Now I need to use the toilet. And there's no point in washing my body in the bathroom. But I'll do it anyway, if only to fill this last hour before shit gets real.

When I pass through the lounge, I see that the bomb is hidden under a blanket, and that confirms that it's finished. Harry made quick work of it.

Spike—thankfully—is asleep in the corner, as far away from the bodies as he can get. I wonder if he was always funny about corpses, like I have always been, or if he developed an aversion in his time with the dark fae.

Even though he's asleep, I take care to lock the bathroom door before I turn on the bath tap. As I let the water run, I do my business on the toilet—grateful that it flushes for me—then strip off.

The tap water is cold, as expected. Not icy or freezing, but uncomfortable nonetheless.

Still, I get to work. Naked and tucked up in the bathtub, I grab a sponge and rub it with a soap bar. Suds gather quick and I scrub myself raw.

After I run body lotion all over me for no point other than to keep myself busy, I comb my blonde hair; natural, a hundred shades of gold and ash and yellow. Gone are the days of sun-bleached highlights and hairdressers.

Once I'm finished pampering myself, I wipe clean the mirror on the wall above the sink. And as soon as I see myself—my wet champagne hair, my ocean-blue eyes hooded with too-heavy lashes, my pale lips chapped by mistreatment, a pointy chin free of blemishes but sharp cheekbones with the faintest hint of freckles—I'm yanked back to a moment in time.

I was standing in my ensuite, staring at myself in the ceiling-to-floor mirror, empty bottles of pills in each hand, a glass bottle of vodka spilling out on the chaise seat behind me.

I blink and steal myself back to the present. A shudder uncoils down my spine. I shake it off.

I redress, starting with my loose underpants and light-pink bra. Grabbing my white country-style dress, I shimmy into it, making a point to ignore the freckles that feel like they are burning against the lace of my bra.

I leave my socks, since they are so worn-out and gross that putting them back on after washing seems futile, and I slip my bare feet into my ankle boots. Then I re-secure the gun in my right boot for easy access later.

Who knows, maybe I'll save the last bullet for

myself?

It's a violent way to go, so different to the stealth of pills, but if it's a last resort…

We'll see what happens.

And when there's a knock at the door and Paul's voice calls out "It's time", I realise I'll find out my fate very soon.

8

And before I know it, we have left the flat and found our way to the cusp of the village.

We stop at the mouth of the main road. The dark fae should be coming up this way soon, if not this very moment.

To avoid the critters, only two torches are switched on. The faint light helps guide Harry down the road a bit. Paul and Mikey flank him. Still it hardly eases the tension in Harry's stiff shoulders. At least he has two others surrounding him if the critters come or the dark fae are earlier than we predicted.

I don't have any such protection. Where are my human shields? Instead, I'm alone, tucked down at the nose of a rusty old sedan.

Peering around the hood, I keep my handgun loose in my grip as if too scared to hold it firmly, and I watch Mikey and Paul veer off from Harry.

Harry is left standing alone in the middle of the road, precariously holding the bundled bomb in his arms, covered by a sheet.

He's left alone only for a moment while the other two push cars off-road. Eventually, the road is a clear path down the middle. The dark fae won't have much of a choice than to take the middle, the path we moulded for them, and then they'll be wandering right into our trap.

Harry sets the blanketed bomb on the road, between two particularly large cobblestones. As per our plan, discussed in the flat before we left, Paul brings over a cardboard box. It's dented and damp enough to not draw any suspicion—looks like any other litter around the streets after the days of evacuations.

Once the bomb is concealed by the sagging box, the guys rush over to us at the mouth of the road. Then, we all move into motion, finding our positions. I have a gun, so I'm made to be closer to the explosion point. Those of us armed with fire-weapons are huddled at the cars cutting into the end of the street, crouched and silent.

Those with knives slip farther back into the shadows—they keep hidden around the corners of the street's final buildings before the road turns to gravel and carries off to the next far-off village.

We have to stick fairly close together for this last stand. It's not like radios work these days, and can't go lighting up the street and betraying our presence. We have to be near each other to know when we need to act and also so we all die around the same time. No need to go drawing out the inevitable.

But then the thought pops into my head, *How many of us will flee?*

My money is on Spike for the frontrunner. Over by the corner of the street, he's clutching onto the wall, pressing his forehead against the rough texture, and his shoulders are stiffer than if he was carved from stone.

That's all I see before a torch flicks off on that side of the street.

He'll run. Or at least he'll do what he mentioned earlier and declare himself a kuri to save his own life.

I won't. I'm ready to die.

I'm twisted, ok, I grant you that, but wouldn't you be tired? We all come to a point in our lives, surely, no matter our circumstance, and are tempted by the thought of a forever calm, quiet end. *Peace.*

I've been at that point a long while, now. Maybe forever, or for as long as I can remember. The thing that is different now is the end of the damn world. No use in fighting to stay alive anymore. Now, my wishes can be fulfilled, and I won't go down alone.

A torch is flicked off, and we're doused in total darkness.

I don't know much about homemade bombs, but I can't decide for certain whether or not the one Harry built is timed or connected to a detonator. Though I highly doubt the detonator since not even walkie-talkie radios are working anymore.

So I go off my gut that it will explode whenever it does, or even if it's disturbed. Not like I can just sneak a glance at Harry's expression in the thick blackness to disprove my theories.

It feels like forever that we are all stiff and motionless in our positions, just waiting. The silence is familiar—and suffocating. It's so thick and heavy that it's like a weighted blanket draping over me, pushing me down further to the ground. Anxiety moths spring to life in my belly. It starts to churn and, in the dark, my cheeks burn hot as nervous sounds start to crackle in my gut.

Faraway, I hear a shuffle of boots, and I'm a little relieved knowing that I'm not the only one who can't keep quiet.

Silence this time around is more uncomfortable than it's ever been before. Probably because we've never been sitting in it, waiting for dark fae warriors to stumble upon us and our bomb before. New things always make me anxious.

Then faint wisps of light start to break the black. I peer under the sedan, hidden behind the tyre, and see the far end of the street start to warm with orange and red hues. Fire-torchlight.

Only the dark fae carry those.

Their kind of fire-torches are different to ours. Those ones never seem to extinguish, run out of fuel, burn down or out, unlike ours. So we're left to rely on the battery-juiced torches to light our way in the darkness.

Not that any of it matters now.

Crooked and bent under the hood of the car, I keep myself shielded by the thick tyre, and watch the street's horizon. The light grows bigger and stronger, climbing up the faces of the thatched houses, slowly beginning to shed illuminance on what brings it to this part of the village.

The tip of the street slopes downhill, so I see the steeds first.

Can't really call them horses, those two hairless, grey-skinned beasts that prickle my skin and shudder my spine. Look more like skeletons with old, aged and leathered skin pulled tight over them. And their tails... razored and sharp, flashing to mind those wretched tentacles that dropped out from the dark and latched onto Jamie.

But those ghastly steeds are nothing compared to the ones mounted on them.

Four of them, just like there were when I watched them be separated from their army. I've seen them before, but never this close, and not with such strong, direct torchlight to light up their faces and shimmer their black armour like pools of tar.

Now, the sight of them does a lot more than spear me with ice-cold stabs of fear. It cuts off my breath, trapping it in my chest, and widens my dampening eyes.

This is really happening.

Even if I changed my mind and bolted into the blackness now, they would hear me. They might even see me with their super-night-sight. And I'd be one of the first to go down.

Now, I look at them and feel warm teardrops roll down my hot cheeks. My breath releases so loudly that I slap my free hand to my mouth and muffle the noise.

Doesn't look like the dark fae noticed, though.

Distracted, they murmur to each other, so confident in their untouchable status in this world that they don't even bother to hide that they are here, small in numbers, perhaps vulnerable—as vulnerable as dark fae warriors can be.

Two steeds, four warriors mounted on them, so six beasts in total. That's what I'm staring at, six creatures from the darkest pits of hell.

Each of them wears the same black tar-like leather, a sheen that glistens off the torchlight. Their physiques, while all muscular and strong, do differ—I can tell that even from this distance. The front two, the ones leading the steeds, reins in hand, are the broad-shouldered ones.

Holding up the fire-torches, the dark fae behind them look narrower, but by no means less intimidating with the inky scars running over their faces. Or are those tattoos? It's hard to tell through the distance and adrenaline pumping through me.

But I do notice the warrior at the front right, the one closest to me. Maybe that's why I notice him. I like to think so. It could also be that, when he twists around to look closer at something he spotted in the shadows, there's a giant gap at the back of his strappy armour.

In place of the missing inky leather, there's lightly-bronzed skin pulled tight over rippling muscles. His bare back is lined with thick holster straps and, most startling of all, two thick, crooked scars mirroring each other; they run from the middle of his shoulder blades all the way down to the small of his back, exact replicas of each other.

I wonder fleetingly if the scars were intentional or a wicked, thought-out torture from another.

Then he turns back around, facing me all over again, and something flips deep in my belly. I loathe myself in this moment. I've seen a lot of dark fae before from afar and hell if they aren't all absolutely beautiful in their wicked, cruel and brutal way.

But there's something about this one...

It's a different beauty. One that steals me.

His skin is olive-oil. That's what I notice first, glistening in the warmth of the fires.

Then my gaze flickers to his hair. Cropped, tousled and parted at the side, each brown strand is so dark I would think them black if it wasn't for the faint chocolatey shimmer dancing over them. His eyes, reflecting amber in the torchlight, are downcast as he leads his steed alongside the other down the street. Long lashes cast spidery shadows down his bronzed cheeks, and his plump lips are pulled into a tight line.

He knows something is off. But he isn't prickled or alert. He is utterly calm—at peace, almost as though he wants this.

It floods my veins with icicles, and I loosen a shuddering breath. My palm muffles the sound, but still, his eyes snap up ... and he stares right at the car I'm crouched behind.

A violent tremble rains down me; even my scalp

tingles. I'm utterly motionless as I keep my wide eyes on him.

Faintly, I catch the twitch of his full mouth. A half-smile. He lifts his head until he is looking down his nose on the car and his eyes are almost out of my narrow line of sight.

Out the corner of his mouth, he mutters something to his companions. They sharpen, gazes darting all over, suddenly restless. They think it's just humans waiting for them, ready to attack. I'm absolutely certain they suspect nothing about a bomb—

Because they still are headed right this way.

9

Their pace is so agonisingly slow that I wish to Mother Earth and all of her brutality that they would hurry the fuck up. I can't keep fighting off this adrenaline pumping through me much longer.

But they are drawing closer to us and, even from under the hood and the dark fae faces starting to lift out of sight, I catch the glint of amusement in the striking one's eyes. If it weren't for his poker-straight posture and broad, set shoulders, I would think him utterly at ease with the softness to his expression, his free hand resting on the thigh of his leather trousers and the other holding loosely onto the reins.

He looks unperturbed. Not troubled in the least.

And yet, there's a hunger burning in the amber hues of his eyes—and it's more than just the firelight reflecting off them.

Something crackles to my left. I cringe against the hood of the car, my breath swelling in my chest, and cut a glare into the thick black. But I don't see what made the noise. I only know that it came from the direction of Harry and Paul—maybe Mikey, if he's still there. Knowing him, he's probably slipped around to a new position, thinking he's in *Mission Impossible* or whatever. Good guy, just a bit away with the faeries.

Well…

I shake off the irony and loosen my breath, quiet and slow. It shivers a little, but nothing too audible and, after a few breaths, I'm able to find a steady, silent rhythm again. Those damn breathing exercises they taught us at school to "cope with panic" and all that.

Hey, I'm not dissing it. That shit works—sometimes. Can't always get the chance to stop and breathe.

But I do have a few moments to centre myself and breathe while I wait for the dark fae to reach us.

I throw another peek under the sedan. Beneath the metal guts of the car, I see only the hairless, bony legs of grey steeds—they are mere metres from the bomb now.

But they split around the box.

My heart drops, sinking all the way down to my bum.

I watch as the two steeds peel away from each other and—*clonk-clink-clonk*—clomp around the box planted in the middle of the road.

The icy disappointment unravelling throughout my body is too much like the anxiety rising up in my veins. A battle of emotions, and yet a numbness engulfs me and I bow my head in defeat.

Guess we'll have to fight with just our hands, knives and guns. Won't do much damage that way, but it's all we have.

I was just hoping that the bomb might give us at least a chance—

That crackle comes out again. I blink, looking up at the darkness just as a faint light flickers on; a torch.

Harry stands there, his blotchy face streaked red and white with tears, and he swallows back something thick and emotional. His mouth twists into a grin-snarl hybrid and he slowly raises a gun that I just now realise is gripped in his trembling hand.

My heart stops in my chest—and it's all the time I have before Harry fires the gun right at the bomb in the middle of the fae-steeds.

A wink of silver speeds past me just as he pulls the trigger—and a dagger sinks right into his chest.

It happened all at once—the gunshot, the dagger, Harry is dead, and the bomb….

Boom!

I barely have a moment to flatten myself to the ground.

First, I'm aware of the sudden screaming in my ears. No, not screaming. That's ringing. I hear nothing but a high-pitched whistle; a kettle left on the hob too long.

My hands slap onto the back of my head. I stay crouched, body folded in half.

Distantly, I'm aware of the cries—the shouts of surprise. From our people or theirs?

A cloud of debris and shattered cobblestone is tossed through the air. It envelopes up, pulverised stone raining down on my back. I can hardly draw a breath that isn't dusty and ragged.

Burying my face into the crook of my arm, I struggle for clean air. Every muscle in my body is bolted like balls of lead, and I wait—it's all I can do. I wait for the cries to subside, the thick cloud to disperse.

I wait for the first of our group to switch on a torch. Whoever aimed light at the bomb has turned it off now. But the fae have torchlight and the bomb will have started fires, so it must be the cloud of dust I can't see through, not the darkness I'm so used to.

The longer I'm forced to stay tucked to the ground, the more I'm regretting this fight. It's not that I don't want to hurt them or send them to their deaths, but it's the violence of it all. None of this will be clean.

There will be blood and guts and throats and organs just flying about all over the place, and that means that in my final moments, I'll be the one vomiting. My final breath will be of stomach bile, I know it.

The thought has me cringing, my face twisted into a grimace, as the noise around me starts to fade away. It's only now that I realise the ringing in my ears has gone faint—still there, but soft enough that I can hear the shuffle of boots on the road, the squish of what definitely sounds like flesh and blood, and a whispered groan ahead—one of the dark fae.

So now I know. We at least got one of them with the bomb.

Oh fuck, I hope the steeds aren't suffering. As ugly and cruel-looking as those things are, I pray to Mother Earth that they were taken out quickly.

I can't be seeing anything like that. I'll never stop throwing up, the image will never stop haunting me.

Starting to forget why I agreed to this in the first place.

Oh, that's right. I'm fucked up and I want to die.

The cloud starts to thin.

The dust is settling.

My sight is returning.

A torchlight flickers on, not that we need it. After the blast, fire has been left burning on the road, and the dark fae have dropped the fire-torches they carried—or they have been thrown away from them in the blast. Whatever the reason, brightness comes in oranges and reds, and it floods the street.

A heavy sigh billows out from me, coming from deep in my belly, and I push to my feet. Movement shuffles all around me.

Everyone is creeping out of their hiding spots.

Before I straighten up, I wipe my sweaty palms

on the skirt of my dress, then fix the gun in my grip. My hands tremble like leaves caught in angry wind, and I can't unwind the coiled stiffness in my shoulders.

The punch of my frenzied heartbeat has found itself lodged in my throat, choking me. I swallow it back as best I can, but it does little good.

And I can't delay it a moment longer.

Paul has cocked his shotgun and gone sprinting onto the spill of the road. Mikey shadows him, close to his heels, and jumps over Harry's corpse as though it isn't there at all.

Did they know, I wonder? Was it a part of their plan that, if the dark fae didn't disturb the boxed bomb, then he would be the one to shoot at it? Because I don't remember him ever having a gun before the moment he aimed one at the bomb.

My question is answered when Mikey doubles back and pries the handgun from Harry's death-grip. Too soon for rigor mortis to creep into his body, but his fingers are all tangled around it and the trigger.

He's too careless with prying the gun away, but he manages, and then he takes off again after Paul.

Laura is next to sprint past me. Then another, and another, and they move in shadowy blurs in my peripherals.

I can't look away from Harry.

The dagger is sunken so deep into the split between the ribs that even the leather-wrapped hilt looks to have burrowed into him a bit. Blood so dark that it's almost black in the shadows spills out from the wound, making a spreading, swelling puddle on the ground.

Feeling my face drain, I turn my cheek to the body and let my lashes flutter shut on the swells of nausea rolling over me.

It's the blood—it's always the damn blood and guts, but never the death. Guess that's why I'm a pill-taker and hider, not so much a cutter or a killer.

Distantly, I hear shouts and cries reignite. There are calls for me—my name ringing over the clashing sound of blades and the blasts of gunshots. But it can't be helped—my body heaves forward and a spill of brown-murky bile flows out of me. Never good to puke on an empty stomach.

I spit out the last of the taste—my mother would have a fit at what I've turned into in these dark ages—and wipe my mouth on my shoulder. Best I can do with a battle raging on back there, meaning that at least one of the dark fae survived well enough to fight.

I'm dreading to find out exactly how many still live.

Reluctance turns my legs to stone, stiff and heavy, as I push up from my crouching position. Slowly, I force myself staggering closer to the road, to the glow of orange firelight illuminating the bloodbath ahead.

Two of the fae are dead, or at least knocked the hell out … with some limbs missing. It was the two fae at the back of the steeds who are limp and partially delimbed on the road. I spot a muscular leg, naked and covered in wet-like black ink across the road on the pavement.

With a shudder, I force my gaze away from it. But then my focus lands on the steeds. At their rears, they have practically been gutted by the bomb. Their insides are now outsides, and all over the cobblestone.

That queasiness hits me all over again.

I can't do this.

I can't.

And yet, I have little choice.

Still, I manage one stumbled step forward before I'm thrown with another violent heave. Another wave of sick rolls out of me. Brown splashes on the ground and droplets hit my boots. I spit again.

I shudder and readjust my sweaty hand on the gun limp at my side.

"*Lee!*" Paul's holler punches right through me, calling my name. "*Coralie!*" he bellows, over and over. The panic in his voice forces my gaze up, and I see a massacre.

Two dark fae survived. I know because only two bodies (or parts of them) are on the road.

But I can only see one and he is putting up a hell of a fight. I throw another look around the street, but I don't catch any sign of the other dark fae—the one who had captured my attention earlier. Maybe his body was blasted too far away, hidden behind a car or something.

The one fighting is really in bad shape. There's a gaping hole burrowed in his lower back and gashes all down the side of his neck. And still, he's slaughtering us.

My group has him surrounded, but with a sword the length of my own leg, none of them can get too close. A young redheaded boy tries, and with a manic laugh, the fae swings out the sword almost lazily, and takes the boy's throat flying through the air.

Using the moment with his back turned, Laura jumps forward with a huge hunting knife. She manages to lift it up high for only a heartbeat before the fae swirls out of the way and boots out at her legs.

She crashes onto the road. A blink later, and the tip of his sword has plunged into her forehead.

She dies instantly.

"LEE!" Paul hollers again, the boom of his voice rippling through my body.

It's enough—it's all it takes for me to kick into action. I sprint towards them, jumping over the nauseating pools of blood and the severed leg of a fae, until I'm skidding to a stop at the circle of survivors.

The dark fae swerves around. His wild green eyes land on me, alive with a blend of rage and bewilderment. He didn't expect this. Maybe, like his missing companion, he expected a ragtag group of humans to put up a fight. But he definitely didn't expect to be one of the only survivors of his group.

Loosening a shaky breath, I lift the gun and fix its aim on him. He moves for me, his upper lip curling to bare sharp teeth—the kind made for tearing out skin. Before he can take another step, I hear the *chk-chk* of a shotgun.

Paul takes his chance.

He aims the barrel at the beast's back and—

He fires.

The blast is strong enough to have the fae stumble. But he doesn't stop. His snarl rips out with a viciousness that curls my toes in my boots.

As he turns on Paul, I shoot out at him.

Then again, another gunshot … but not mine or Paul's. This one comes from Mikey. There should be one more, from Spike. But I don't see him anywhere.

The dark fae loses patience. There are bullet holes littering his back and sides. With a violent roar, he swings out his sword, spinning his body around as he does.

First, I just see a spatter of blood stain the air. It seems to hang there, indefinitely. Then as suddenly as it came, it shoots out across the road and I feel some specks hit my cheeks.

I blink, stunned.

With that one swipe, he took out most of our group. Guts and chests are severed, wide gashes—completely irreparable—appear on those struck and, after a shocked moment, they all go crumpling to the ground.

Only Paul and Mikey are left standing. They stand further back now after jumping out of the way.

We are the only survivors—assuming Spike wasn't killed somewhere in the dark.

Mikey fires again from a safer distance. But the click is all that comes, no blast. He is empty.

The fae turns on him, his snarl twisting into a vicious grin.

Mikey is the one to take charge. He drops his weapon, trades it for a knife stuffed into his belt, then shouts out a war cry I've only ever heard from armies of dark fae.

He runs at the fae.

And just as the sword is brought down on Mikey's head, splitting him right down the middle in one swift swipe, both Paul and I fire our weapons until they are emptied-out.

Mikey's two halves slap to the ground.

The dark fae looks down at him once, blinks, then looks up at me, a question furrowing his brow. Confusion clings to him—maybe a touch of awe, too—before he drops the sword. It clatters to the ground.

That's when it all starts to bleed; the gunshot wounds that litter his face, the hole carved into his back from Paul's shotgun shells, the wounds from the bomb. It's all too much.

And he falls down, too.

Silence sweeps us. There is nothing content or relieved about the quiet. It is thick and tense, suffered with mourning.

Finally, Paul and I lock gazes. It's only then that I realise I'm weeping. Tears roll down my cheeks, streaking the blood spatter there. I can taste the metallic coin-like flavour on my mouth.

"There's one more," I whisper, telling him the worst possible truth I could in that moment.

It took how many of us to take down just one? And now it's just us two left, and one more of them.

Hopefully he's injured enough that we can take him out easily.

But I know in this dark, new world, for us humans, nothing is ever that simple.

10

We checked the rest of the groups; both the fae and our own. All are dead. Their wounds, too severe to be left more than a few seconds before death sinks in. There's no one left to save.

Now, we hunt.

The search for the other dark fae—the one who captivated me on the steed, the one with ribbed scars running down his back as though he once had wings that were cut off, and whose eyes are black firelight—is a gruelling search. For me, at least.

Paul and I split up to cover more ground. We stay within the confines of the firelights, cast by the discarded fae torches (that never seem to burn out) and the flames leftover by the bomb, clinging to cars and evacuation leaflets.

It's a grim hunt for the last fae.

Pools of blood have started to congeal into dark, almost-black puddles with lumps dotted around them. I come across at least two severed legs and one arm.

The chunks of the horses fuck me up the most. Even if those steeds came from another realm, they are animals—and I was the type to have horses at our estate in Germany. Although, I never visited all that much given that my parents wanted to keep me in boarding school as often as possible.

Still, it's not easy to step over chunks of their guts on the road. I might have stopped to heave a couple of times, but my stomach refuses to throw up some food or even bile. I have none left.

I honestly didn't think I would make it far

enough to be included in this search. But by slipping into freeze-mode when it all went down, I suppose I bought myself some time.

Thank you vomit, I think bitterly. My weak stomach is both a blessing and a curse, just as life is these days.

For me, the search brings out something more than nausea. I find him—not the fae. I find the coward.

Spike is half-tucked under the hood of a white, rusted van, just his boots and bum sticking out.

I kick out at him. The toe of my ankle boot catches him on the bony part of his ass. He jolts, a squeaky sound catching in his throat.

I'm not the bravest person going around these days, *but Christ*, what is this guy's damage?

"Get out of there," I grumble with another kick, this one more forceful than the last.

He mutters something under his breath, but he doesn't budge.

With a sigh, I drop down to crouch by the hood and tug my bag around to my front. I change the clip of my gun for the half-full one. Four bullets left. Won't do much, not against the last fae (if he even survived). It took two guns and a shotgun to bring the last one down.

Aim for the head, is all I can think to remember. Body shots don't seem to do much to them, barely slows them down, just pisses them off.

I hope the dark fae is dead. And I have a thought—if he is dead, and we find his corpse, and I have four bullets left … I can finish this for all of us. Four bullets, three survivors, me, Spike and Paul—and the dark fae.

Spike curls up tighter.

"There's only one left, if he's still alive" I tell him.

"And we need you if we're going to finish this."

I hear a faint sigh before he shifts. Crammed under the hood, he manages to turn around and face me, still curled up.

His eyes are wide; wide and wet and terribly afraid.

His bottom lip trembles as he whispers, "Down there. He's down there."

My veins turn to ice. The cold runs down my slackening face, prickling my body.

Slowly, I lean to the side and peer down the edge of the van.

And there he is—the missing dark fae.

He is lodged between the faded firelight and the darkness, planted in the shadowy corner.

Holding his hand firmly against his side, he leans back against a shopfront. Looks like the bomb blew a hole just under his right ribcage. Black blood spills out of his wound, coating his bare fingers.

Lashes drooped low, it almost looks as though he is sleeping; passed out, maybe. But then they flicker. As lead bolts to my gut, I realise that he *was* passed out for a moment, but now he's recovering, now he's waking up … and now he is turning his head and looking right at me.

Dark eyes burn beneath his low-hanging lashes like embers on charcoal. And in his amber-flecked eyes, there is only murder and bloodlust, and nothing else.

I should have been one of the first to jump into action back there when it all kicked off. Because that way, I would have been one of the first to die. I would have gotten the quick death I wanted.

Now, with those dark dangerous eyes on me, I know that a quick, painless death is not written in my stars. This fae is going to skin me alive, gut me like a fish.

His hair is dishevelled from the explosion. Dark-brown strands hang over his forehead and brush against his brows, adding shadows to his already cruel stare.

Tingles rain through me at the sight of him. And those tingles spear into rising panic as he pushes himself up from the wall. His mouth twists with a pained grimace, but his eyes possess the fire fuelling him.

He isn't going to make this pretty.

He staggers a step and relief swells in my chest that he's too injured to fight—but then I realise he is merely scooping up his dagger from the ground. It's a narrow, crooked thing, about the length of my forearm, but the tip glints with the dangers of its sharpness.

Instinct kicks in. I call out for Paul and grab onto Spike's arm.

I yank and pull and heave and shout until Spike has no choice but to roll out from under the car.

Maybe I want to use Spike as a shield, or some form of distraction. Maybe I want all of us to go down.

I'm selfish, I know that—but whatever my intentions, it doesn't work out for me, because when I cast a cautious glance back up, the fae is already storming towards me.

I stagger back. The heels of my boots catch on Spike's feet and I fall back on my bum, hard. My wince is muffled with a panicked cry as I kick out my legs, skidding away from the advancing fae.

Spike scrambles to his feet. He throws a look back at the dark fae—then ducks. He just drops to the ground, hands up, in complete submission.

Fucking coward, spineless rat.

I'm about to be gutted and all he can do is throw his hands up in surrender. He's going to pull that kuri-card he was rambling on about earlier. And I'm going to die.

It's the plan to die, just not this way. I let myself hope for a moment that it might be a quick death, or even that I might be able to blow my own brains out. But with this massive—and I mean tall, looming, towering—fae storming towards me, blood spilling out of his side, I know that I'm a fool to let hope trick me.

Where the fuck is Paul?

Just as I think it, bootsteps come stomping down the road.

I crane my neck enough for it to ache and I see Paul running into the circle of torch-light. I look back, breath hitched.

The dark fae pauses. He lifts his gaze to the newcomer and, slowly, a snide line flattens his mouth. His lashes lower and I sense in my churning gut that he knows Paul was a frontrunner in what happened to his people—he might have seen with his own eyes Paul shooting at his comrade.

Maybe that'll deflect some of his rage Paul's way. But I can't be ok with that, because Paul isn't like Spike. Paul is what so few people are—*good*. By my standards, anyway.

Can't let Paul take the brunt of the wrath. We have to go out fighting, even if Spike isn't going to help us.

The dark fae strides around me, his blood-slicked hand flexing around the dagger's hilt in his grip. He just passes me before I'm rolling forward onto my feet.

I swivel, lifting the gun with me—and the barrel presses right on the dark fae's spine, inches beneath his shoulder blades. Fuck, he's tall. Over six and a half. I'm not short. 5ft6, but I feel fucking miniscule behind him.

His height makes him all the more terrifying as he freezes, rage seizing up his body, and stands perfectly still for a heartbeat.

Paul has skidded to a stop on the street. His shotgun is all out of shells, so he holds a dirty, bloody knife in his hand—the kind looted from butcher's shops.

Everything and everyone is totally silent.

My finger slides over the trigger.

I start to squeeze—

The blast of the gun splits the air.

My eardrums are ringing, screaming in my head, dizzying me. But it's more than the gun that throws me into vertigo. The dark fae spun around a microsecond before I pulled that trigger, and fuck he's fast. He swerved quickly enough for the bullet to spear into his shoulder instead, then he's suddenly facing me.

I manage a moment to blink, stunned, before his massive hand snatches my throat. His grip is so tight that my eyes bulge. His other hand reaches for my wrist and he twists, hard. Something snaps beneath the bruising skin—bone, a fracture maybe.

My scream is mangled by the grip on my throat.

The gun falls from my hand and hits the road.

And I'm faced with him, his fine nose a whisper away from mine, his breath chilled and crisp against my mouth, and the sheer power of his rage radiating from him and sinking into my icy bones. Curls of dark-brown hair make a dishevelled mop atop his head, making him look all the more fierce, very much as though he's in the middle of a bloody battle.

And isn't he? I don't have much fight left in me,

but there's still Paul—creeping up behind the fae. Unarmed, I'm less of a threat apparently. He doesn't kill me. At least not yet.

He clenches his teeth, dimples digging in deep to his sharp jawline. He spins me around—my feet dangling above the road, kicking out when I summon the strength, my face turning purple and blood pulsating through my ears. And he slams me against the back of the van.

My head cracks off the window. Eyes rolling back, I feel my muscles relax one-by-one. A haze settles over my vision. I see only shadows as the tension on my throat eases, and I crumble to the ground.

I blink, lashes heavy over my eyes as I force my gaze up at the shadows. Paul slashes out the butcher's knife, but it only cuts air. The dark fae leans back just in time to avoid the strike.

Then before I know it, before I can even warn Paul of the dagger, it is plunged upwards through the underside of his chin. The dagger is so long that I can see the gleam of it poking out from the tip of Paul's head.

My lashes flutter as a sickly spell washes over me. Goosepimples have plagued my body with shivers.

Still plunged in my daze, fresh blood spills down the back of my neck; I have a head-wound apparently. Mutely, I force myself to crawl forward, my trembling hand reaching for the discarded gun on the road.

I loosen a choked sound as my fingers touch the warm metal, and I have it safe in my hand again. I don't look up at the dark fae to see if he notices me or what I'm doing—I hear the dagger be ripped out of Paul's head, then the slam of his body hitting the ground.

As fast as I can manage, I loop my finger around

the trigger and roll onto my side. I aim the gun up at the shadow—the shadow that's starting to clear in my sight.

With his back to me, I can better see the damage of the bomb. The cut on his side is wide, gaping, and near-black blood spills from it, soaking his black leather trousers. The belt of weapons secured around his waist are slick with blood—both ours and his own, likely.

And those scars have darkened; black and leathery, something that reminds me of the skin that bats have stretched over their wings. But these are just magical scars from another realm where my people don't belong, and whose people don't belong here.

The fae turns, his back muscles rippling as he moves, and my gut flattens with a newfound weight. Fear chokes me as his ember eyes land on me—then shift to the gun I have aimed right at him.

Aim for the head.

Aim for the head.

But the damn fae knocked my head against that van good, and it's all I can do to keep the gun aimed up high, let alone aim it perfectly. My hands are trembling too much for a steady shot.

Then, I pause. I fucking falter, and it's my mistake, my error to bear—because he gives me this look, this flat-mouthed, grim look of bother. Lashes lowering, he bows his head, releasing a soft sound that is faintly reminiscent of a sigh, and keeps his gaze on me.

It's almost as though he doesn't want me to shoot at him, not for himself, but for me … as though he doesn't like what he'll have to do.

Of course that's insane. He's a dark fae warrior and this is his calling. Murder, blood, gore. It's in his bones.

I pull the trigger.

The blast is something I'll never get used to—nor his speed.

He twists, I shoot again. He twists—and I have two bullet lefts. I shift my aim to his head and shoot. And he ducks. I shoot again.

It takes me a moment to learn if I even hit him. The last bullet definitely missed—it's gone off to the other side of the road. But the first two ... there are two fresh streams of blood coming from his shoulder that tell me I did hit him, just not where I wanted to, and not anywhere close enough to save myself from torture.

He rolls his jaw, his gaze cutting down to his shoulder. Almost leisurely, he threads his fingers through his hair, biting down on the inside of his cheeks, then drops his hand to his side.

He looks at me from beneath those thick, dark lashes, and my insides chill instantly.

Then in a blink, he's moving for me.

11

I have barely a heartbeat's time to scramble to my feet. The head-wound has the ground swivelling beneath me, and my feet unsteady.

Still, I'm standing—barely—and I stagger up to the pavement.

Distantly, I'm aware of Spike's voice as though he's shouting out at me, saying something or other, maybe warning me that the warrior is right behind me. But I can't hear much else other than the blood pulsing behind my eardrums. And I know I can't outrun him.

So why do I even bother?

Survival instincts, maybe. Whatever it is, I stumble into the wall, using it as support to turn myself around. Then, I'm spent.

My lashes are drooping as I look ahead and …

The dark fae is just standing where I was when I shot him. In his hands, he turns the dagger around, over and over, and he considers me with a molten gaze fuelled by magma.

Slowly, he tucks the dagger away in his weapons belt.

Then he's storming towards me.

I cringe back against the wall before the first hit comes—and it does. His fist catches me right in the gut; a choke seizes my throat. I double over, eyes rolling back, and time stands still for a moment. Just as I'm about to drop to the ground, his hand balls up again and he brings it down on my spine.

The force knocks me to the pavement. I don't hear the slam of my impact, but I feel it burning all over my body like fire.

I'm sprawled on the ground, face-first. Cheek pressed against the rough little gravel-stones, tears dampening my cheeks.

Please make it quick.

One dagger hit to the back, right where my heart is, and it'll all be over.

I don't beg, what's the bother of it? I don't want to keep on living this brutal, dark life.

Just please—be quick about it.

Of course, I shot him. So there will be nothing quick about this.

I'm flipped onto my back and, for a moment, I don't know how. Then I feel the explosion of pain on my side; cracked ribs from his brutal kick.

My back arches and my arms wrap around my middle. A silent scream twists my mouth; as though all the sound inside of me is silenced. Even now that I want to scream at the top of my lungs, I can't—I can't make even a whimper.

Nothing.

Is this dark fae power? Is he doing something to silence my cries?

I don't know what I'm thinking—it's the head injury. It must be.

Maybe when he was choking me, I lost my voice completely. And now I can't scream as he stands over me, running me over with a suddenly detached look. His mouth has flattened into a grim line again.

He starts to blur as tears build up in my eyes. I look away, turning my cheek to him, arms and legs spread, ready for the final blow.

And my gaze lands on Spike.

Though glazed, I can see that he's watching,

wide-eyed. He trembles like a leaf in a storm, hands still raised.

Didn't bother helping, not even once. Not me, not Paul, not anyone.

I knew I was right about him.

After a while, the dark fae traces my stare. Spike seems to sense this. He jolts his arms up higher, alert, and his mouth moves. I can't hear much, but I do catch the alien word 'kuri'. He's telling him all about his freckles. And he shows him the freckles, too.

I don't look back at the dark fae, so I don't see his reaction. All I know is that Spike has been forgotten for now, and instead, I'm the focus once more.

As he steps over me then lowers to straddle my middle, my face twists with a fresh wave of silent sobs.

This is it. The end I've been craving since I hit puberty.

Teeth clenched, I close my eyes. But my heart doesn't hammer. It's perfectly calm. *Ready.*

I hear the zing of a knife being drawn from his belt, feel the shift of his weight on my bruised ribs. My groan is silent, still trapped under his spell.

"She's a kuri, too!"

The shout rips through my entire being.

My eyes snap open and I stare up at the dark fae and his hardened face.

"She is!" It's Spike, calling from the van. "She has the freckles—see for yourself, they are on her right breast!"

Cheeks aflame, a whole new fear rises up inside of me.

Something dark and moody passes over the warrior's face. His ember eyes shift into pits of blackness, and he stares down at me. The short knife in his hand—with a blade the length of my middle finger—betrays that he meant to make me suffer, to draw out my death.

After a long, terrible moment, he brings the wide edge of the knife closer to me until I feel its cold kiss against the side of my neck.

His voice is low, thickened by an unearthly accent as he says, "Show me."

Instantly, I shake my head. The gesture frees trapped tears that are now rolling down my temples and into my hair.

"He's lying," I try to say—but no words come out of my mouth. Silenced, still. Then, I suddenly feel the pressure in my throat lift. It comes out of me in a choke so forceful that it jolts my body against the fae straddling me.

"Repeat," the warrior growls.

I manage a croak, "He's lying." Sounds as though I haven't spoken in years and moths and dust have lived in my throat. Feels like it, too. "No freckles. None."

But of course he can see the faint ones on my face.

His eyelashes lower over burning black eyes. In the fading firelight, amber flecks dance like glittering threats.

"Lies," he mutters, then he ghosts the blade down my neck.

I arch away from him, but it only invites the knife to cut over my throat. He passes over it, though, and moves down to my right breast.

I freeze. My fingers clench, toes curling in my boots, and a rigid ghost possesses me. Can't move. Want to move, want to fight. But can't.

Is this fae power again?

The blade slices suddenly, and a wince catches in my throat. I look down my body to where the knife cut; right between the bodice of my dress. The gash is long enough to reveal more of my body than I would ever dare to in front of a dark fae—or anyone.

Veins turning to ice, I shudder a breath and, finally, break free from the stiffness that plagued me. Is it instinct that has my hands flying up at the warrior's face?

I claw out at him, my bitten-down nails doing nothing at all. But I switch my aim for his eyes—I don't get the chance to connect before his large hand snatches up my wrists then slams them to the ground. He pins them above my head, the bones screaming in protest.

Undeterred—as though I hadn't fought at all—he reaches his other hand for my ripped bodice and yanks back the material. My bra is revealed, and it's a hammered heartbeat before he's tugged it down and shown my entire breast.

Tears are spilling out of me now. My face twists with a stifled sob, but it escapes anyway and jolts my body. He pays me no mind.

Tilting his head, he clearly sees the three dotted freckles down the side of my boob. He considers the marks for only a moment before he's pulling up my bra to shield me. His weight is lifted from me a moment later, and the aches in my ribs can finally breathe.

He stands over me, his dark eyes shifting between me and Spike who hugs himself closer to the van.

Then he lands his gaze on me. "You can be useful."

With that, he storms off to the middle of the orange-glowing street. He reaches for the bloody remains of a steed. For a beat, I watch him—I'm still sprawled on the pavement—snatch up leather satchels and water-skins and ropes.

When I blink out of my daze of shock, I roll onto my side. A groan rumbles through me, but I push through it and manage to get onto all fours.

"Get down," Spike's urgently hushed voice snares out at me.

I shoot him a scathing look meant for murder before I shakily get to my feet. But that's as far as I get. Don't get the chance to run or free or stab myself in the neck with a discarded weapon.

The dark fae is marching back towards me, two satchels bundled in one hand, the other hand loosely holding onto a coil of black rope.

He moves for me first, not so much as glancing at Spike still tucked up by the van. He's not a flight risk, but I am.

The warrior snatches my bruised wrists. He's quick to bind them with the black rope—which I notice with a wiggle is far smoother than our rope, but as strong as handcuffs. Then he drags me over to Spike.

In silence, in utter and absolute defeat, with tears streaming down my face, I watch it all happen but I don't really feel any of it. We are both tied to his weapons belt with the rope, he slings the satchels over Spike's neck for him to carry, wraps fabric around his middle wounds, then moves through the remains of the massacre that happened here.

He pauses at every human body, running a dagger through their hearts as if to ensure they are dead—or to collect their blood in some sort of cultural tradition, maybe. I don't give it much thought.

Feel like a zombie, just moving because I must. A

zombie in tears.

Then he picks up a lit torch and hands it to Spike for him to carry—looks like he's the mule. I flicker my gaze down to my body and it's clear why I've not been given anything to carry.

Besides my torn bodice and the bruises on my ribs hidden by my dress, my legs are scattered with cuts and bruises, and there's a thin stream of blood coming down my left arm from my head-wound.

And still, I'm alive.

I don't want to be alive. I never wanted this—to be captured, to be a slave. I wanted to have a dagger through my heart or a bullet through my head.

Without much heart in my voice, I mutter, "I'll kill you the first chance I get."

It should be enough for him to snap my neck.

Instead, the warrior turns on me. Firelight dances in the tarry blackness of his eyes and warms his beige skin-tone. He looks down his narrow nose at me, his strong jawline clenching tight, and he puckers his mouth in thought.

He moves in a blur, leaning forward. I jerk back as he snatches the hem of my dress and—tears a strip right off. He's standing again, shoving the material into my mouth, then winding it all the way back to the wound on my head.

I frown—he's muzzling me and yet binding my head-wound at the same time. Surely a coincidence.

And my plan for a quick death has failed all over again.

So when I get the chance, I won't do what I promised him. I won't kill him. I'll just take my chances and slit my own throat. If I can take Spike down with me, all the better.

And sooner the better, too.

I shot this dark fae twice. His shoulder bleeds because of me. I threatened to kill him, hell I *tried* to kill him.

Just because of some stupid freckles, I'm still alive. But that sure as shit shouldn't mean I'm safe.

No, I'll be made to suffer for what I did. And I'm just not cut out for torture, you know?

I need to think of a way out of this, and fast.

I can't be the slave—*the prisoner*—of a dark fae warrior.

I won't.

end of book 1

DARK FAE: EXTINCTION

DARK SKIES
BOOK 2

QUINN BLACKBIRD

DARK SKIES
BOOK TWO

I

I'm a prisoner now. Captured by a dangerous dark fae warrior.

Just an hour ago, I watched with my own eyes as he struck a dagger up through the underchin of a man who was the closest thing to a friend I had in this world.

Just an hour ago, I should have died alongside him. Instead—even after shooting this dark fae, trying to kill him as he has killed so many of my kind—I am still alive. Taken by a dark fae beast.

And I'm not alone.

Spike is with me, too. 'Kuris', he called us. That we both have a set of three freckles in a crooked line is what makes us kuris. Whatever that means, I have no clue—I only know that it spared my life when I wanted to die. I wanted to go out with the rest of my group.

I'm tired.

So, so tired of it all. The hiding, the running, the fleeing, barely scraping by on tins of nearly out-of-date foods we find in dusty old shops, forever quiet streets and villages, the dangers lurking in the dark, the fae armies hunting and burning us to ash, and the latest danger of those tentacle-creature clouds that took some of us out before we even had the chance to take our final stand.

Can't you see I'm tired? That I don't want to be here, trapped with one of those beasts? It's not a salvation of any kind to me. Salvation comes in pill bottles and bullets to the brain, not in slavery.

I can't do this.

Already, my heart is jumping up into my throat, trying to break free of the confines of my chest, my eyes burn with the eternal sting of tears, and it's all I can do to keep my shallow breaths steady enough to stop myself from spiralling into a panic attack.

I need to get the fuck out of here.

Or I need to kill this beast trapping me.

Either way, I need to be free.

2

I'm dying all over again. This time on the inside.

I ache for the burn of vodka down my throat and the warmth of a pill-bottle in my grip. Instead, I can only feel the prickly sensation of thirst burning me, and all that my hands touch is my side as I twist my arms around to my bruised ribs. The rope around my wrists doesn't allow for more than that.

This warrior, this dark fae—my fucking captor—has no intention of letting us go, or even delivering us a swift death. He means only to make us suffer.

At the top of the gravelly road, where the land lumps up into a mound, the warrior stops us—and he makes us look down at the fiery road of the small village. He makes us watch for a time too long at severed limbs and pools of blood, all glistening under the flames of bomb-fires and a leftover torch.

The fire is spreading, reaching from the insides of abandoned cars and jumping across the road to the wood-faced houses bordering the street. It isn't terribly long before we're watching limbs and corpses burn.

I can't help it. The sting of stomach acid crawls up my chest and settles in my throat. It bubbles there, preparing to throw me into a heaving fit.

I shut my eyes and look away, as though that will somehow prevent the mess I'm about to make all over the gravel. But I hardly get the chance to steady myself and fight off my climbing nausea—

A large, warm hand snatches my face. It clutches so tight that I can feel white spots blossom all over my aching jaw as I snap open my eyes.

I meet the ember-glare of a furious warrior.

The dark fae looks down at me, his lashes low, his eyes burning like the flames down the hill. His bowed upper lip twitches as he snarls at me, "Watch."

Yet, he makes the decision for me. His fingers dig harder into my face, pushing out my cheeks and lips until I resemble a goldfish, and he twists my head back around to face the village below.

I blink away tears I didn't realise had come.

After a few thrumming heartbeats, his hand slips away from my face. It's then that it hits me—the smell, no *the stink* of burning flesh.

And now it really can't be helped.

My body is thrown forward with the force of it. Instinctively, my hands reach for the fabric strip bound around my head. I wrestle it out of my mouth just in time.

Faintly, I'm aware of the warrior's hand snatching the back of my neck, as if ready to yank me back to him, as though he thinks I'm making a run for it—but then that wretched gurgling sound happens, and it's quickly followed by a splash of brown bile.

Dazed, I watch droplets splatter onto my boots. Who cares? They are already beyond saving, with dried blood, cuts and scuffs, earlier traces of vomit. I've only made them a bit worse.

It's my dress I'm worried about. The torn hem at the front wears a faint brown stain that reeks of stomach acid. That will be hard to wash out with some pond water we might come across—if I survive long enough to let the smell bother me. Maybe I'm getting ahead of myself.

But then, this is what they do, isn't it? The dark fae.

From what Spike told me—and what I saw with my own eyes in the army during the earthquake—it's clear this warrior has taken us as slaves. Spike, with the two heavy satchels slung over his shoulders, weighing him down to the left and the firetorch in his sweaty hands, he's the mule.

But if he's the mule—what am I?

Can't think about that.

Just a flash of gruelling possibilities in my mind throws me forward again and I collapse to my knees. Kneecaps crunch on the gravel; my wince is drowned out by another spray of sick. This time, spatters reach my bound wrists and curled fingers.

A grimace twists my face just as a shudder runs down me.

The warrior has no patience for my weak stomach; I feel the rough tug of the rope before it takes my wrists out from under me. With my support lost, I fall to my side, barely missing the puddles of vomit on the gravel road.

I throw a glare up at him. Hatred masquerades as bravery as my lip curls and I spit out the last of the sick from my mouth.

He is unfazed. Shadows from his long lashes crawl down his face, partly illuminated by the growing fires down in the village. He tugs again and I have only a split second to propel myself up onto my bottom before I can be dragged across the vomit.

Spike keeps his gaze downcast. He looks at the toes of his boots, silent and utterly submissive.

Maybe I should be more understanding of what his fear manifests into within him. My fear isn't healthy either—it turns me into a suicidal wreck. The anxiety that boils up inside my veins, rising like a pressure cooker, floods me with urges to run at the warrior and sink my fingers into his eyeballs.

Of course, my fear doesn't make me entirely stupid. I'll just receive another punishment—another beating, maybe. And I can't take anymore bruised ribs or aching back pains. So I'll bide my time.

Gritting my teeth, I force myself to stand. Upright, I sway for a heartbeat under the watchful stare of the warrior. Those ember eyes are just begging to be ripped out of their sockets.

He keeps his grip tight on the black, smooth rope that binds my wrists to his weapons belt. His other hand, though, is pressed firmly against his side; challenging the blood flow that seeps out from his bomb-wound. And his shoulder leaks black streaks—littered with bullet wounds that I left in him.

Fleetingly, I wonder if I've been punished enough for shooting him. The kick to the ribs, the punch to the gut, the knock to the back, the kidnapping; surely that would be plenty revenge for each of the two bullets I shot into him?

I fucking hope so.

My body is screaming all over. I can't handle another moment like that.

And still, the nausea clings to me as I sway between Spike and the warrior.

Spike simply hugs the satchels closer to his chest, as though he fears my little episode of sick and retching will bring punishment down upon us.

The warrior just watches me for a long, quiet moment. That moment is broken as his gaze drops to my belly and a crease knits his dark eyebrows together.

I wear a frown to match his and trace his stare. There's nothing there, other than vomit-and-blood-stained patches on my dress.

His eyes flicker away, landing on the sick crawling over the small gravelly stones. And then it clicks in my head like a light switch turning on.

He's wondering if I'm pregnant. He wonders if my sick spell is from fucking pregnancy—definitely can't be from the stink of burning flesh in the air, right? Bloody fae. So ingrained in violence and horror that they can't even fathom the idea of a human finding all that gore absolutely sickening.

"It's the smell," I tell him. "If you were normal, you would be sickened by it all, too. Psychopath."

Amber eyes snap to me, alive with the flames on the torch and those burning the village to ash. The creases on his brow fade away and he reaches out for me. He grabs the fabric strip from around my neck and lifts it; it fits snug in my mouth, silencing me.

I lower my lashes on the devil before me.

The warrior suddenly turns his back on me—and the gesture has my ropes tugging with the twist of his belt.

I stagger forward as Spike is quick to right himself.

He marches on up the gravel road, and we follow with little other choice. Though, I do writhe my wrists in the rope for a while, but there is no give, not enough space between the rope and my skin to even stick a pin through.

Before we walk out of seeing distance from the village, I throw a look back over my shoulder. It still burns. And I recall that the dark fae warrior moved through the corpses and stabbed them all, making sure they were dead—or collecting their blood for his dagger, like some sort of ritual or whatever.

There were bodies missing. Back at the village, among all the smog and the blood, I was sure of it.

Now, I'm not as certain. Could just be my head injury, perhaps I'm simply confused. But when we walked the road for corpses, I counted two less than what there should have been. Kale was among the missing ones.

With the warrior so close to us—and having a clear knowledge of our language, apparently—it's not as though I can ask Spike if he noticed, too. So the moment we have a chance to talk, I'll make note to ask him.

As we walk the gravel road, far beyond the village's orange hues and into the darkness with only the torch to shed light on our steps, I hold onto the possibility that others survived, that two of our group got away. Because maybe, just maybe, that means they might come back for us. They might devise a plan to save us, or do what they can to end the warrior before he does *godknowswhat* to us.

Wishful thinking, though.

If anyone did make it out of the village, they wouldn't come back for us. We would be left behind, and I know that. It's sort of an unspoken rule among our group; those who fall behind, stay behind. Don't risk more people to save them.

So I feel the cold, hard truth that we are alone, and this is our fate.

Still, there is a glimmer of hope. The warrior is hurt. His wounds bleed freely; especially the one on his side that, no matter how hard he presses his hand against, oozes black—the worst kind of blood. He's slowing down, too.

I watch him out the corner of my eye, how his shoulders are starting to slump, and his fingers are slick with black blood. The firetorch casts orange glows over the gradual stagger of his legs.

Before he can succumb to his wounds, the dark fae takes us off-road and onto dry, cracked land. *A farm*, I think fleetingly, as we step over a fallen wire-fence.

The walk over the farmland is hard on the knees. The earth here is tougher than rope, harder than stone. Part of the reason I'm wearing a dress is that the breezes are warm and the air is dry—it's undeniably summer, and the heat has dehydrated this farm.

I've never understood how, without the sun, we still have seasons down here in the dark. Without photosynthesis, how can the grass and trees still grow, how can the air be touched with warmth?

But then, the dark fae have a magic about them, don't they? A power untold, undiscovered by my kind. Maybe the sun really is penetrating the black in a way, but we just can't see it?

The thoughts dizzy me. At the back of my head, the wound there is throbbing. Feels like it's swelling, as though I can track every step it takes to turn into a large lump.

I wouldn't mind so much if it weren't for the rest of my body. Aches have sprung up all over, and I will be surprised if when I look at myself, there aren't bruises littering my pale skin.

And even though the warrior has slowed down from his own injuries, he's still moving too fast for me across the desolate farmland. I'm struggling to keep pace—and when the toe of my boot catches on a small rock, I'm sent tumbling over.

Long blonde hair is quick to whip my cheeks as I go sprawling; a tangled mess, blinding me. Skinny arms grapple to stop my fall, but t's all I can do to cross them and block the impact.

I land hard on a collection of stones. My cry of pain catches in my throat as a grunt, muffled by the material silencing me.

There is no pity to be found in the dark fae. He jerks the rope hard enough to have my bones screaming in protest. I swear my wrists *creak*.

Again, I cry out, feeling the tug reach all the way up to my shoulders.

Bastard, my eyes say as I struggle onto all fours.

Weighed down by satchels and balancing a firetorch in one hand, Spike stretches down for me. I think for a moment that he's meaning to help me up, but the creep grazes the side of my breast as he reaches for my arm.

My muzzle garbles the words I throw at him but not the kick that I boot out at his calf. He grunts at the impact, his balance thrown off for a beat.

I push up from the stones.

As I right myself and shake my wrists to ease the aches budding there, I catch the gaze of the warrior. His frown has returned, cutting his gaze between me and Spike.

I cast my stare down to the stones, avoiding him as best as I can.

The rope loosens somewhat. I lift my eyes up just enough to watch as the warrior unwinds it a little from his belt, feeding me more space.

My face wrinkles with a scowl. He must need me relatively well and healthy to be a useful slave to him before he finds his army.

Whatever his reasons, I'm given no more time to mull them over—he's walking again, and I notice that he's cut to the left. Purpose sinks into his steps, alleviating some of the stumble he had earlier, and he journeys into the thick black ahead.

He's seen something. We're coming right for it.

And with the rumble spurring deep in my belly, I pray to Mother Earth that he's found something to eat. I'm starving, and I don't recall the last time I ate other than the chocolate nougat bar back at the flat.

I'm so hungry I could eat the rotting sheep carcass we briefly pass.

And then we come to it; what the warrior saw ahead in the dark—

A shed.

The warrior swipes the torch from Spike (he trembles at the close contact and I recoil). He doesn't pay any mind to our reactions, probably used it by now after carting around so many kuris with his unit.

My eyes blur as he flips the torch so that the flames lick up it, not flicker above. He sinks the small fire into the hard earth.

Light is extinguished, and we are thrown into bleak nothingness.

3

Still, even after years of this life, I'm amazed at just how dark it is out here. It's a thick blackness, *dense*—almost suffocating. It's more than air; it is a smog, blinding and tangible. I can physically touch it; feel its soft curls against my skin, the pressure of it against my palm.

Can't see my own hand in front of my face.

Hell, I can't even see my nose.

Jolted out of the moment of awe, the warrior marches across the plains to the shed—and the ropes drag us along with him.

Then I hear it and I trip over my damn boots. I right myself quickly, but my heart still punches against my chest. There's a faint *creeeeek*, *hreeek* slithering out of the dark.

For a strangled breath, I think of the tentacle critters. Their *skrt-skrt*, slip and slap sounds. But then I pinpoint the noise; it's coming the ground between me and the fae.

It's only the torch dragging over the coarse earth. Fleetingly, I wonder if it works the opposite way of a match being struck; dragging it over something hard and coarse (like a gravel road) keeps the flames at bay, when it should be the other way around.

We reach the shed—and I know we have reached the shed because, suddenly, the warrior pauses. Before I get the chance to so much as blink, I feel the rope tug and it's quickly followed by a crunching sound.

It takes me a moment to figure out what he's done. Booted down the rotting door, hard enough to split fragments of wood clean off. I mean, he probably could have tried for a handle first or, you know, *pushed* the door open. It's a shed, not like it's all locked up tight.

The warrior slips inside; I hear his soft-soled boots pad quietly on crumbled splinters of wood. No ceremony of ushering us inside, the ropes just wrench us in after him.

Spike and I smack into each other at the doorway.

I throw him a glare in the dark and elbow my way in before him.

Don't care that he's exhausted from carrying all the weight of the satchels and torch, it's me with the bruised ribs and cracked spine (it sure feels that way, at least) and throbbing head.

Besides, I simply don't like him. And I don't feel too comfortable being stuck with him maybe more than with the dark fae. It's an evenly distributed unease, I decide.

The door slams shut behind me, and I jolt with a fright spearing through me. The warrior must have reached back to close it; too close for my liking, since I feel the warmth of a breath disturb my hair as he moves away.

In a heartbeat, light is suddenly flooding the shed. The glare is so sudden and fierce that my eyes snap shut, burning. I cringe away from the source—the torchlight that the warrior flicked upright.

Bringing my bound hands to my eyes, I rub the aches away as best as I can. But even then, as I lower my fists and squint out at the light, it glares against me like sunshine catching on glass. One blink, two, three and four blinks until the shed starts to come into focus.

In the middle of the crammed space, the dark fae is spearing the bottom of the torch into the wood floorboards. The force splits a wooden panel right down the middle, sending cracks all over.

My eyes widen at the sheer power behind that one impale.

I turn my gaze away from him, if only to spare myself the obvious display of his strength. I don't need more to worry about than I already have, thanks.

Beside me, Spike fumbles with the satchels. Desperation clings to his slack, pale face and slumped shoulders; he's dying to drop it all on the floor.

I wonder why he doesn't, but then, he's been with the fae before, hasn't he? So he would know the customs and what is expected of us.

Guess it's safe to follow his lead and simply stand by the rattling door, wind whistling in through the fresh gaps. We wait.

And as we wait for our commands, I look around the shed. Not sure what it was used for, if anything at all. Maybe storage, a long time ago, but it's been looted already? Hard to tell, since it's so sparse in here.

Some damp boxes are piled in the corner, slanting like the Tower of Pisa, threatening to topple over at one gust of wind too strong. Beside them, there's a wood post sprouting from the floor and reaching all the way up to the leaking ceiling. On the post, I notice some rusted hooks, but I have no clue what they are meant for.

Only a bench fills the other side of the cubed shed, with a tin bucket tucked underneath it. On the walls, there are more of those rusty hooks and some ropes, but nothing else that I can see.

What I can *feel* is something else entirely; the icy wind creeping into the shed. It's colder in here than it is out there—or I'm just starting to feel the chilly shift in weather now that we've stopped for longer than a few minutes.

Whatever it is, I'm suddenly freezing. The urge to wrap my arms around myself tickles me, but with roped wrists, I just can't manage it without turning myself into a pretzel.

This summer dress is a blessing for when heat swells through France and pierces the darkness, but come night—without the cardigan left behind at the grocer's shop—it's a curse.

I hunch over myself, arms huddled against my aching chest, and I watch pale clouds of breath escape my trembling lips.

My moment is cut short.

The rope jerks me forward and, as I glare up at the dark fae, I see that he's taking us over to the wood post in the corner of the shed.

With expert fingers, he unloops the silky black rope from his belt, then fastens it to the hooks on the post. Before he leaves us there—right where a gap in the wall is, and the chilly wind gusts through—he takes the satchels from Spike's neck.

I stand there, unsure of myself, as the dark fae limps (and he does limp, now) to the bench. He dumps the satchels to the floor; they land with a thud as he straddles the bench.

Spike is first to move. He slides down the post, back pressed against it, and looks up at me.

With a lurch of the head, he tells me that it's ok to follow suit.

I do.

At least he's useful for something. Sort of—he's quick to lean his head back and close his eyes. How can he rest during a time like this? We're fresh prisoners of the warrior, the one I bloody shot, and he's out for a nap?

I definitely don't feel safe enough for that.

So I'm rigid against the post, watchful of the dark fae as he peels off his strappy leather armour. He lets it fall to the floor before he digs through the nearest satchel to him.

I'm a masochist for watching this. He peels away the strip from his side-wound, and bile crawls up my throat at the raw sight of it. The skin at the edges is torn; completely shredded around a gaping hole filled with black blood and *godknows* what else. Their anatomy never seemed important before. Maybe it's something I should have paid better attention to, since my group failed in wiping out all four dark fae.

Better late than never, I think.

So I force back the bile with a hard swallow, and I pay close attention.

From the satchel, he holds a tiny phial of glittering black powder in his bloody hand. He fights off a grimace as he twists to better bare his wound.

Whatever that black powder is, it's valuable to him—I see that in the way he's careful to tip just the right amount onto his fingertips before he gingerly dabs it around the torn flesh. When he's done, he uses the leftover stains of black on his fingers to—I retch—stick his fingers into the wound and swirl them around.

The retch is so violent that I'm thrown forward and it comes out in a gurgling, burping sound. The fae throws me a withering look, ember eyes burning with anger—he blames me for this wound. Maybe he should. I was as much a part of it as anyone in my group.

Looking away, he pops the cork-lid back onto the phial. But he doesn't put it away in the satchel. For a beat, he considers it flat on his palm. His gaze cuts to the side, where his bullet-ridden shoulder is. Two thin streams of tarry blood run down his olive-skinned chest, passing over his weapons belt.

My mouth flattens into a thin line.

This black powder is magical.

Already, the massive gaping hole on his side is starting to ... *knit together.* As though invisible threads are stitching it closed. I mean, it's slow work, but it sure as shit doesn't escape my notice. How could it?

He decides against using the black powder on his bullet wounds, for some unknown reason. I can't decide, because I can never pretend to understand the mind of a dark fae.

I watch as he pockets the pinkie-sized phial— then he looks at me, and my blood runs cold. Ice spears through my veins at the sheer burn of his amber eyes, firelight dancing off the shadows of his strong jawline.

I stiffen against the post, urges nipping at me to fight against my restraints. There's something dangerous—furious—about the way he's considering me.

My heart leaps up into my throat, thickening and choking me.

The dark fae pushes up from the bench, his gaze never leaving mine, and strides towards me. Already, his limp is gone. His advancement is confident and predatory once more.

I choke on the lump in my throat as he reaches me. Neck arched, aches sprout all over my body as I sink back against the post, wishing it would swallow me whole.

He swipes at me—

I flinch and...

The tear of rope rips through the air.

Peering through one eye, I glance up at him, at his hand. The end of my rope is loose in his grip. He watches me, his brows lowered, and commands one word with renewed strength, "*Up.*"

I don't hesitate, though it fucking hurts, I tell you. Every muscle and bone in my body shivers with cries as I force myself onto all fours, then push up to stagger in front of him.

"Wrists." He makes a gesture, then flattens his palm.

I try not to think about why. I try to shut my mind off and go numb. But the fear pumping through me is keeping me too alive.

Breaths shudder in my throat.

Gingerly, I place my bound hands in his waiting one. He tugs once, twice—then the rope comes spiralling off my wrists as delicately as a ribbon drifting to the floor.

Buds of fresh pain burn my skin. I draw my wrists in closer and rub them. With a curt glance down at them, I see the bruising in the torchlight; like blackened purple and yellow kisses all over my flesh.

I'm given a sparse second to nurse my wounds before he snatches my arm, then drags me over to the bench. He shoves me down onto it. A cry catches in my throat, eyelashes fluttering, as pain explodes throughout my entire body, from ankles to my pulsating head.

A dizzying moment wafts over me. I try to steady myself, force myself upright on the bench.

What does he want with me?

My heart is pounding in my chest, dizzying me more, and my breaths turn short and choppy.

As I blink my blurry eyes open, I see that the warrior has sat himself opposite me, straddling the bench, and leans over to dig through the satchel. He pulls out a loot of bandages and mason jars of salves and balms, then shoves them into my shaky hands.

Are these for me?

It's clear that they are medicines of sorts, and I'm littered with injuries. But—

All thoughts of treating my wounds are swiped out of my head. The warrior lowers his lashes on me, then taps his fingers against his bullet wounds.

"You did this," he growls at me, and a shudder seizes my spine. "You fix it."

My mouth tilts into a grim line.

Buds of red sprout on my cheeks; shame from fooling myself for a moment that I might get a little relief.

I bow my head and let the loot in my hands rest on the bench between us. I turn to straddle it too, facing him. All that twisting around punched too much pain through my back and ribs, and I have to be as careful with my wounds as possible.

Before I pick through the medicines and dressings, I make sure to tug down the torn hem of my dress to cover myself down to the knees. Just in case. I doubt dark fae would think that way about my kind— but still, you never know.

Fingers trembling, I reach for the wooden pair of what looks to be tweezers. Only, this wood is smooth and polished, not a splinter in sight.

I have to remove the bullets first, it's unavoidable.

Only when I try to pinch the slick tweezers in my fingers, do I realise how badly my hands are sweating. Gone all clammy, and the wood keeps sliding against my skin.

I suck in a choppy breath and shut my eyes.

I do what my therapist (the school one) told me. Count to ten.

The warrior is silent and still as I do this; he doesn't interrupt, he doesn't rush me. But I can feel his fiery gaze burning into me as I ground myself, my lips moving along with the numbers in my head.

Finally, my breathing has settled into something mantric, and I lift my tired gaze to his fiery eyes; though the fire has dimmed, and left are pits of mostly black with orange flecks.

Biting down on the inside of my cheeks, I reach the pinched tweezers for his shoulder. The wounds are perfect holes; no torn skin, just holes that have stopped oozing blood. Around the wounds, perfectly olive-toned skin stretches over muscles and looks as smooth as butter to the touch. A spike of jealousy hits me that a brutal warrior can have better skin than I do.

Throwing all thoughts from my mind, I focus on the task at hand. I line up the tweezers with the nearest hole—but I know my strengths and weaknesses; I turn my cheek to his shoulder as I dig into the hole.

For a moment, I prod around until the tweezers connect with the bullet. Smaller than what I would have thought. All too easily, I slip it out and let it fall to the bench. It bounces off and lands on the floorboards.

I swallow back any singe of bile before I aim for the next hole. And I did this, over and over, swallowing back burning vomit, all the while with dark pitch-black eyes watching me too closely.

He shows no signs of pain on his stoic face. Looks like a bronzed mask has slipped over him, and it's aimed right at me. I pretend not to notice for the last of my sanity.

It's only after the last bullet has rolled onto the floorboards that the nausea starts to rise up in my chest. Before, I was battling only bile—but now fresh waves of nausea roll over me like foamy waves take a beach, as I bring a threaded needle to his shoulder.

This time, when I swallow, I can taste the sick rising up inside of me. For a beat, I shut my eyes, hand hovering near his arm, and force pleasant images into my mind; memories of the Alps dusted in early-season snow, Capri and Saint Tropez, yachts and table-dancing and champagne showers.

But it does little good.

I open my eyes and it strikes me like a punch to the gut.

I double over, craned to the side, and spew up mere drops of bile. Nothing left in me to be sick with. Not even water. Fuck, do I need water right now to wash away the taste in my mouth.

The warrior grows impatient. After my third heave, he snatches the threaded needle from my hand and stitches up the wounds himself. Then he smears a beige balm—the same tone as his skin—over the holes.

I right myself, my eyelids drooped, and use the back of my hand to wipe any bile from my mouth. It takes me some moments to fight off the sick.

Watching me, he wipes his fingers clean on the bandages between us.

He reaches down for the second satchel. As he plants it between us, I get the chance to scoot back on the bench, putting some safe distance between us. Well—what is safe? I'll never be safe with him.

But for the moment, I won't be terribly hungry either, I learn; he pulls out a lump of baked bread, mostly eaten already. The lump is about the size of my balled up fist.

And he hands it to me, his jaw tight, and his lashes lowered. I trace his gaze as it cuts to Spike at the post (who is apparently awake now, and watching us too closely) then back at me. *To share*, his eyes tell me.

Hesitantly, I take the bread with shaky hands. He doesn't snatch it back, so I bring it closer to my chest, as if to shield it from him, protect it.

Before I can bite into it or split it in half to share, he's snatching up rope and grabbing my wrists. I wince sharply.

His grip loosens and a frown pinches his brow together.

He watches his work as he fastens my wrists together, then rises from the bench. Slowly, he takes me back to the post, keeping a pace that my aching body can manage.

Once he ties me up to a hook, he makes back for the bench, leaving me with Spike in the silence, broken only by the crackles of the torch.

I split the bread in half.

Spike's hungry gaze follows the hard lump as I hand it to him. He snatches it with as much greed as what lights up his muddy eyes, and he's quick to bite into it.

I drop down beside him and nibble on the edge. My experience in this new life has taught me that, after a sick-episode, don't eat so fast.

Apparently, it's meal-time for the three of us. The dark fae fishes out some bread from the satchel for himself—and a jar of damp strips of meat, sort of like fish or fermented green ham. Super fucking gross. At least it doesn't smell. I don't think my weak stomach could handle a stench.

I'm finished my meagre ration before the warrior has eaten half of his healthy spread. He's dug out more; something that I suspect to be some sort of nut-like cheese, and berries so black that I'm certain they are poisonous.

Spike shifts onto his side after a while, his back facing me. He tries to sleep—and I mimic him.

Maybe it's that I haven't slept in well over some days or that my entire body feels as though it's been hit hard by a bus or that I ate something filling for the first time in a long while, but my eyelids are fighting against me. And I'm losing the battle.

As I lean against the pole, drifting off to a world where monsters haunt me just as they do here, my fear creeps into my thoughts—is this my life now?

Before, I had every intention of working out some way of killing this creature. But if I'm tied up all the time, watched so closely, I doubt I'll ever get the chance to go through with it.

The next option is to kill myself. But again, how and when?

I hate myself in my final conscious moments before sleep; I should have used those last bullets on myself. I shouldn't have let the adrenaline drown me, take me for a victim. I got so caught up in the moment that I couldn't stop to think.

I should be dead.

But I'm not. I'm resting against a post in a windy, whistling, icy shed, prisoner to a dark fae, and a massive creep beside me who might try to cop a feel while I'm asleep.

Still, despite all of that I do find sleep.

Sometime during, I wake to turn sides. That's when I'm faintly aware of the warrior hunched over on the bench, reading a map.

He cuts his gaze to me.

I turn my back on him and a mist takes over me.

I don't want this life.

4

Warmth brushes against my hot, sweaty cheek. The sensation draws me out of my sleep. I blink awake— and lurch back.

Spike has scooted much too close to me during my rest, and he *watches* me. My widened eyes land on the one breathing too hot on my face.

I've reeled back, horror slackening me for a frozen moment.

Distantly, I note that in my peripherals, the dark fae is spread out over the bench and he sleeps. And that gives me an opportunity.

I hike up my knee, prepared to deliver a precise boot to Spike's face. But before I can even twist my face into a snarl, he holds up his hands, one finger lifted, and shushes me. His gaze cuts to the bench, to the sleeping fae.

The message is written all over his hopeful face. He was meaning to wake me up, waiting for the warrior to fall asleep.

I shift, leaning my aching—definitely bruised— side on the post. Letting my head rest on the rotting wood, I mouth, "*What?*" with more snark than maybe the question needed.

"Kale got away," he whispers, and my heart stops.

The scowl that I wear starts to fade away, wrinkles turning to smooth lines. I sit up a little stiffer.

I knew I counted someone missing from the scattered corpses. Well, I'd counted two people missing—but head injury and all that.

My voice is hushed and rough, as though I haven't had a sip of water in days. *Have I...?* "You're sure?"

"I saw him run," he tells me, all secrets and leaning closer—so close that I can smell the sleep-stink of his rotten breath.

I pinch my mouth shut. Try not to breathe.

"It doesn't matter," he adds with a glance over his shoulder at the motionless fae. "He won't do anything about this..." With a jerk of his head, he gestures to us and our situation.

"I'm only in this because of you," I hiss before I even know the words have sprung to mind. That missing scowl returns, twisting my face. "If you hadn't said anything about my freckles, I would have died back there."

His furry eyebrows knit together. "Is that really what you wanted? He wouldn't have made it quick, Coralie. I've seen how long they can draw these things out. And sorry, but I didn't want to watch that. Not again."

'Trauma' creeps into my mind. Flashbacks of what he might have experienced and seen in his time with the dark fae army.

But fuck his trauma, he's only created mine in avoiding his.

"I wanted to die." My voice is firmer now, all hushes crushed to dust. "You stole my choice—and that's just the kind of guy I think you are."

His furrowed brow smooths out. A mask slips over his face; stony. "I'll remember that," he promises, then shifts around to turn his back to me.

He leans against the post, as though to find rest, but the tension in his shoulders alerts me that he's still very much awake, and absolutely fuming.

Perhaps I should be more concerned about his promise—or threat, more like. Maybe I should I worry myself over it but, in truth, I think there's little he can do. We're watched too closely by the dark fae; so little opportunity to set each other up.

And, in all honesty, anything he does that might deliver me to my death is a blessing and I welcome it.

Bring it on, little weasel.

*

Sleep is long gone for me after Spike's stinky, hot breath woke me up.

For too long, I've stared at the orange glow cast over the wooden boards above me, then rubbed my fingertips over the burnt-sun rust on the hooks I'm bound to. Eventually, I can't fight it anymore and my gaze lands on the cardboard boxes in the corner.

Everyone else is asleep.

The fae hasn't stirred on the bench, and I fleetingly wonder if that black powder stuff takes it out of him, or he needs to sleep to help recover from his quick-healing wounds.

Spike is snoring, a gravelly sound, so I know he's out cold.

Who's to say anyone will know if I sneak a look into the boxes?

I try my luck and twist around the post to face the boxes. Casting a glance over my shoulder, I see that the others are undisturbed. The rustle of my ropes didn't stir either of them.

Arching away from the post, I stretch out my left leg. Kisses of pain bud all over my kneecap; I snub the pain, since it's nothing compared to the hot, widespread ache that's grown all over my back.

Automatically, my tongue sticks out the corner of my mouth. Under the weight of the aches, my leg starts to twitch the farther out I stretch it. Still, I manage to catch the heel of my boot on the edge of a damp, soggy box. It's nearest me, not on the pile, and sagging—so that's the one I target.

Hitching my breath, I hook my boot into the mouldy cardboard corner and pull my leg back to myself. The softness of the box makes little sound as it drags over the floorboards.

I quit while I'm ahead. No use dragging it all the way over to me and risk waking up the psychopathic warrior on the bench. Or the rapey creep sleeping on the other side of the post for that matter.

Scooting my butt over the floorboards, I shuffle myself closer to the box, meeting it halfway—as far as the ropes allow with some leeway still left over.

Delicately, I peel off a slice of wet cardboard. But at my angle, I'm blocking the inside of the box, and I see nothing but shadows. Could be a horde of rats or spiders in there, for all I know.

The thought spears me with an icy sensation that chills my spine and I twist away. Torchlight floods the interior of the box. And at what I see, a small smile dares to tilt up the corners of my chapped mouth.

I reach out my restrained hands for the top of the pile.

Old photographs, stacks and stacks of them. Most of them gleam a dusty brown hue under the firelight.

I pull out a handful, then angle them towards the torch. I flick through them. Nothing spectacular—if family memories and the memories of our soon-to-be extinct species are unspectacular. Still, none stand out to me. The poses are stiff, faces are unhappy, clothes are too corseted and miserable.

I set the photographs aside before I reach into the box again. I feel around, go through stacks of pictures, until I come across a smaller hard-wood box.

Inception, I think to myself, and that stupid smile twitches again.

I bring the smooth, polished box to my lap, then flip open the golden clasp. Inside, a bunch of medals shine up at me. War medals and memorabilia I assume. Tucked beside them is a small stack of Polaroid pictures (really, one of my favourite cameras).

Now *this* is what I'm talking about. Sincere moments, captured and forever preserved in time—two mates in tank-tops passing a bottle of beer between them; a wedding photograph in black and white with one of those lacy vintage style gowns that I just *love*; and one of those classic ones with a woman leaning up against the side of a train to kiss her lover who hangs out of a window to reach her.

I pinch all three of the photos, tucking them into the side of my boot. With socks, they would be better secured, but I make do.

Those Polaroids flood me back in time when I got my first camera. Same camera (obviously my devices advanced over time), and my first love.

Photography is an eternal passion of mine; one lost some time ago. But in all truth, I was never any good at it. I just did it. I loved my pictures of bland, withering flowers, and shadows stretching over cobblestone streets, and that time my mother passed out in the bathtub after too much morning-vodka. No one liked my photos, except me.

Wonder where they are now. I had a collection, boxes and stashes of them. Probably burned to the ground by now.

I let go of those thoughts as I close the lid on the box and push it away from me.

I tuck back to the post.

As I twist around to face the door, a shadow catches in the corner of my eye and I stiffen. Eyes widening, I slowly slide my stare to the bench—and see the warrior straddling it, sitting upright, and looking right at me.

His arms, bare like his chest, looks slick under the torchlight, as though slathered in tanned oil. Orange light licks up the profile of his olive-skinned face, catching the cutting shadow of his chiselled jawline. Those amber flecks in his eyes dance like wild flames through towns, made darker—more threatening—by the loose strands of dark hair brushing over his brow.

I swallow, audibly.

I have a thought—are all the dark fae so beautiful because they used to once lure us humans into their realm?

That's how the stories go, at least. Could be zero truth to them at all, but I doubt that since most of the world had lost their belief in the fae and then, *what-da-ya-know* (as my school roomie used to say), they came here with all their power and magic and ferocity, and they decimated us.

Loosening a quiet breath punched with exhaustion, I turn my gaze down to the fae's side.

Reddened and bruised, the wound looks nearly knitted shut by invisible threads. He's almost fully healed.

And he caught me in the act of preserving some of human history.

Yet, he does nothing. He says nothing. He simply watches me.

I sink back against the post, bringing my knees to my chest, holding his ember gaze.

After a while, he pulls his gaze from me and starts to check his wounds. I finally loosen a strangled breath and let my head fall with relief.

He works in silence for the better part of an hour, reapplying salve and balms, redressing his shoulder. I take the chance to check my own.

With the dark fae distracted and Spike snoring like a foghorn, I lift up the torn hem of my dress. Revealed, my legs are bruised and scraped from the knobbly knees up.

I cut a glance at the warrior, making sure he's still distracted—and he is. He has his back to me now, hunched over (back muscles rippling with every move of his arms) as he riffles through a satchel.

For a beat, I study those charred-like, ribbed scars running down his back; shoulder-blade to the defined muscles of his smaller back. The scars are exact mirrors of each other, and I still can't decipher whether they mean something in his culture or he was simply born that way.

I throw the scars out of mind. I have my own mending to do.

Knowing it's safe for a moment, I lift up my dress to check my torso. And it's covered in kiss-bruises. Except the right side, where the bastard booted me onto my back and *definitely* cracked a rib or two.

I let my dress fall back into place before I reach up my aching fingers for the strip pulled tight around my mouth. I wrestle it out, then settle it over my nose; it's a better angle to press against the wound at the back of my head, and I can breathe much better this way.

As I look up at the bench again, I catch the dark fae watching me. He has a waterskin in his hand, his gaze burning into the muzzle I fought out of my mouth.

All he does is toss the waterskin through the air. I watch it arc towards me, then land right on my lap. A perfect aim.

Hesitation clings to me. For a moment, a battle erupts inside of me; is it poisoned or is it drinkable water? But then, I want to die and I want to drink.

So what's the harm, I decide?

I pull out the cork-lid and lift the leather-bound waterskin to my mouth. Leaning back my head, I pour a steady stream of tepid water down my throat. Don't even stop to swirl it around my parched mouth.

Barely have a moment to lower the waterskin from my mouth before hands snatch it out of my grip. I snare my snarl on Spike as he starts to guzzle down as much of the water as he can—

But he hasn't got another moment before the warrior is towering over us. One look from the fae, and Spike's hands tremble as he draws the waterskin away from his mouth. He offers it up to the dark fae.

Before he takes it, he shoots a puzzled look at me—that I have no idea the meaning behind—then stalks off to the bench. For a heartbeat, I almost let myself wonder if we'll have more time to rest. But those hopes are shattered as he scoops up the satchel straps then flings them across the shed at Spike.

The warrior storms over to us.

Numbly, I watch as he unloops our ropes from the hooks, then fastens us to his belt. The leeway is shorter now, but I can't decide whether he meant to keep us closer to him, or it was just done without much thought.

Once we're secure, and Spike has the satchels over his shoulder, the warrior adjusts the sword slung over his back and the weapons belt low on his hips.

He makes to move away, but pauses in front of me, turning his head to cast his dark stare down at me. Then, after a moment, he snatches the fabric from my face and fits it back into my mouth.

My face crumples, making no effort to hide the glower I shoot his way.

Indifferent, he turns his back to us and kicks out the door again.

Time to go. And my whole body screams at the idea.

5

I suspect we spent too long in the shed, because the warrior moves faster across the farms this time. Though, he doesn't have his bleeding, gaping wounds to slow him down this time.

Still, it very much feels as though he's trying to make up for lost time.

I'm slow, staggered by the aches that plague my whole body, and he often has to tug my rope to hurry me along. Unlike before the shed, he doesn't pull the rope hard enough to bruise my wrists any further.

The trek is an agonising, monotonous one. Spike fumbles with all the baggage and the torch he has to mule across the plains, and I'm just trying not to collapse on the hard earth. At least the warm breeze is back to warm away the prickles on my bare legs. A small thing to be grateful for. It's the little things these days, you know?

When the dark fae stops in the middle of an abandoned farm—the countless ones we've passed through since leaving the shed all those hours ago (at least a whole day)—he pauses and turns his head to the right.

I study his profile as it hardens; his face turning to bronzed stone. He lifts his strong chin for a moment, then I see the deep inhale he takes through his nose. It fills his chest and spreads out his broad shoulders. When he releases the breath, his body relaxes as though tension unribbons through him, but his eyes lower and he cuts his head to the left.

An uneasy wave curdles my gut.

He smells something—he maybe even sees something far in the darkness. Whatever it is, he knows something's off.

A sudden decision strikes through him. He cuts to the right, our ropes staggering us along behind him, and heads off in the opposite direction to the one he glowered at.

Humans, I wonder? Enough for them to be a threat to a lone dark fae warrior? I mean, he likely recalled how we blew up and killed his companions, ready to die for our cause, and just decided it wasn't worth the risk. So he takes us deeper into the black, and we wind up slipping into a sparse tree-line.

Not the fucking woods.

I hate the woods.

They are so damn dangerous these days. More than they were before. Animals from all over Europe moved wherever the wind took them with the loss of humans; and now, even in France, we have bears and wolves to worry about. Not only that, there are all sorts of problems that come with the dark (and the creepy crawlers!).

Last time my group went into the woods, we wandered right into the path of another tribe's cabin. We lost three of our own trying to escape. Some people are really hungry these days—and humans aren't off the menu.

Gruelling shit.

So it's no wonder I start to drag my boots across the foliage-dusted ground and tug on my ropes.

Impatient, the warrior turns on me sharply. The torchlight reflects off his vexed eyes.

I stumble back a step as he reaches out for me.

His grip is firm as he takes my rope in his hand and guides me closer. Then he loops it around his belt a few more times, until there's hardly a half-metre between us.

Venomous words build up in my throat, threatening to spill out onto my tongue—but I'm muzzled like a fucking dog, and so all I can manage is narrowing my eyes on his unfazed face.

He heads back into the trees; and the pull of him is suddenly stronger the closer I'm bound to his belt. I have little space to fight against him; so, I stumble at his heels, a moody look on my downcast face.

After a while, Spike's breathing takes a hoarse, haggard turn. He's weak; hungry and parched, struggling to carry the load of a mule.

The fae does nothing to aid him. And even if I wanted to help Spike, it's not like I could do much. My body is too broken and bruised to carry anything, let alone a satchel filled with waterskins and food and medical supplies and whatever-the-fuck else this beast has with him. Probably the decapitated heads of his enemies, the psycho.

Despite his choppy breaths, Spike manages to keep pace. And we walk for a long time.

I swear we've been moving for a whole day and night by the time I hear it; a crunching sound to my right, like bone being pulverised.

My heart stops and, instinctively, I duck closer to the side; tucking myself between the fae and Spike, as though they are special shields made for me.

The warrior pauses and looks over his shoulder at me. My wide eyes meet him. He blinks something weary, then slowly turns his gaze to the side, where the crunching sound crawls out from again.

The fae reaches back for the torch. Spike releases it with an audible sigh of relief. But the relief is short-lived as the warrior extends his arm out and, with it, the light of the torch, showing us what's making those noises.

I pale, instantly. I feel all the colour drain out of my face, down my body, and the swirl of it all in my watery gut.

It's a pack of at least five dogs. Pet dogs—old, torn and bloody collars. Dogs that were once loved. And they are feasting on the body of a lone human. Clothes have been torn from the now-exposed body, but it's clear that it was once a man from the body parts that still remain. A torso and bits of meat still clinging to bony legs.

Suddenly need to be sick again.

I shut my eyes, the woods spinning around me, and pinch my mouth shut. My hand comes up to my burning throat. I lean forward, meaning to fold myself over and steady myself, but my forehead touches something cool and firm; the warrior's bare back.

Before I can jerk back from him, it happens; I wrench the gag from my mouth a split second before I'm sick all over the foliage; bits of bark, twigs, weeds and grass, all splattered with brownish, lumpy liquid.

Well, there goes my bread and water.

I blink away the last rolls of nausea—and I realise what I'm doing. I'm learning my head on the fae's shoulder blade.

Again, I blink, this time startled. Then I slowly peel my forehead from his skin and avoid his gaze; he looks over his shoulder at me, a frown pinching his brows together.

Stepping to the side, I clear my throat before I spit out the last of the vomit in my mouth.

He's still watching me, so I just look down at the foliage.

It's not like I meant to lean on him for support. It was an accident, but by the intensity of his stare, you'd think I'd jumped on him and kissed the soul out of his body.

Finally, he pulls his gaze away, and relief falls out of me in a light breath that deflates my shoulders. He shoves the torch back into Spike's hands, then sets off through the woods again.

I keep up just fine this time, pushing myself to my limits. Gotta avoid any more attention thrown my way after that.

It's when we're walking—leaving the dog pack behind us—that it hits me. That bastard wanted me to be sick! He purposely pushed the torchlight into the scene to reveal it to me, all so that I would suffer that bit more.

Oh, I'm so going to kill him when I get the chance. I'll kill us both. Quick and clean. Poison, maybe.

Just waiting for my chance.

I'm not the type to steal a knife from his weapons belt and plunge it into his back. Too much gore, too much blood. And there always seemed to be something personal about a knife, something intimate in a sick and twisted way. I'm more of a poisoner, myself. Sneaky, deadly, and without much gore.

6

Though he has mostly healed from his wounds—the bullet holes are puckered now and the gash down his side, once gaping, is now a mere slit—the warrior still seems to sense a vulnerability.

Perhaps he feels exposed, I wonder. Without his comrades to flank him, with how easily (to him) we took out three of his own kind, it would be understandable that out here, *alone,* his confidence might have been shaken.

So when we reach a small commune—whose village sign is overgrown by moss and the vines of a nearby tree—he cuts his pace down from a stride to something slow, stalky and soft-footed.

This place is more like a suburb than those stunning medieval villages I've watched burn to the ground.

I make no effort to hide my watchful gaze. I study him as he creeps down the edge of the street, his dark eyes sweeping from window to window, door to door, alley to alley.

He takes no chances of being seen if other humans are out here somewhere. At the first sign of a deep street, he cuts off from the main road and heads out of the centre of the town, far into the circle of houses.

Spike adopts the fae's quiet-footed steps. I'm the bull around here, the heels of my boots scuffing off the tarmac, the weight of my agonised body dragging me down. Can barely stand up, let alone keep good posture and move like a panther.

Light is extinguished. The warrior took the torch from Spike, then flipped it downwards; all the flames suffocated somehow, and we're submerged in utter blackness.

I inch closer to the pair, as though that will somehow offer a hint of protection. How twisted is that?

We are led down the curled road of the court, darkness our only companion. I listen to the silence of the world around us. No birds chirp, no rustles of leaves as a breeze passes through, no shutter of blinds or creaks of doors.

I think we are completely alone here. This place is as abandoned as the last village we were in after it burned to the ground from our own bomb.

Ropes tug me to the left.

Blindly, I follow the soundless bootsteps off-road until beneath my soles grass softens my scuffling. Heading up to a house, I suspect. And my suspicions are confirmed when I hear the rattle of a door handle.

Luckily, the door creaks open. I hate the sound of a door being booted in, and I know that would have been his next move if it hadn't been unlocked.

He slips inside, my tight tether pulling me in close behind him. Spike shuffles in after, and as though he knows what to do, closes the door gently. There's a soft click before the torch is flipped back up and orange light floods the inside of the house.

It's uh ...

Well, it's modern. *Contemporary*. Not a favourite style of mine. Reminds me of our family apartment in London. Cold and clinical, little personality or feel of the people who live (*lived*) here.

From the lobby, where a runner rug leads all the way up a corridor, everything else is open-plan. To the left, the lounge (filled with white leather couches and armchairs and a black-marble fireplace. I hope the fireplace works.) stretches through an open arch and into the kitchen (black marble-top counters, stainless steel fridge, rigid stools and a high-tech cooker).

I glance down the corridor that narrows ahead, but it only seems to lead to two doors, one on either wall. Perhaps a toilet and a study. Then I look up at the hard-wood staircase that lines the left wall, leading to the second level, where all the bedrooms and bathrooms likely are, and hope springs in my chest that one day I might reacquaint myself with a warm bath and a fresh change of clothes.

No such luck, of course. I'd be a fool to expect otherwise.

Loosening the longer rope, the warrior cuts a dark look at Spike. "Close the curtains."

There's no hesitation. He drops the satchels to the rug where they thud at my heels, then rushes to the open lounge. He draws the thick, heavy curtains over the window before he's rushing to the opposite open-plan kitchen and pulling down the shutters, then tugging the curtains in place.

The wide space is submerged in only orange-red light from the torch.

As Spike wanders back into the lounge, travelling his gaze around, the warrior stalks over to the fireplace, dragging me alongside him. He tosses the torch into the fireplace—my heart skips a beat and it's all I can do to fight the smile daring to creep onto my face—then unfastens my rope from his belt.

With a curt gesture to Spike, he summons the mule over to us. My once-skipping heart plummets to my churning gut as soon as I realise what the fae is doing ... Fastening my rope to Spike's. Then he ties us to the pillars at the archway between the kitchen and lounge, keeping us secure—keeping us from running should we be foolish enough to think we have the chance.

Still, the disappointment of being fastened to Spike is quick to fade as I lean against the column. I start to slide my back down it, dropping to the floor, and a pained sigh escapes me. Every ache and muscle in my body suddenly relaxes, and it brings an addictive blend of pleasure and pain.

The fae blinks, watching me, before a frown crinkles his arched eyebrows. The corner of his peach mouth tilts down for a beat, then he's turning his back on us and stalking through the house to the staircase. He takes the steps two at a time with his long, muscular legs.

When he's out of sight, Spike and I are struck with the same idea. Instantly, we both scoot around the pillar, aiming our bodies at the fireplace. The hearth is alive with flames now. Fire caught, just as it does in villages, and now a roaring fire is quick to warm us.

Most of the 'dark day', warmth is in the air. But then comes the 'dark night' and it brings chilly breezes and prickled skin with it. So I'm cold to the bone, and this fire is a blessing in more ways than one.

It's been so long since I've *enjoyed* a fire. Seen plenty, of course. Watched them burn village after village, spread through cars and towns, stuck on the top of torches. But it's been well over a year since I've actually sat near a fire and felt that stinging heat burn my skin—and it's fucking *bliss*.

Some might even say it was worth surviving just to experience this moment one last time.

Not like we could have lit ourselves many fires out there in the dark. We used torches to guide our way when we could, or gas cooktops (that did little for warmth), but actual fires?

Not a chance.

That's a signal to others that we are there—smoke, light, flames; all of it could have led anyone right to us. And as we learned as a group, no stranger is a friend. All are foes. And it's a better risk of hypothermia than meeting unfriendlies.

There's something soothing about the fire—and the absence of the dark fae who disappeared upstairs. The hot burn on my cheeks has my lashes fluttering and my head lolling back against the hard pillar. Not exactly the most comfortable position there is, but it's still enough to lull me into a light sleep.

My rest is disturbed after a few minutes or a full hour—it was one of those sleeps, where it's just impossible to tell how much time has passed. But I do know what wakes me—

The heart-fluttering sound of running water. Tap water. *Bath* water.

Coming from upstairs, too. So the dark fae must suffer the same wishes as I do, to bathe in warm water and let the heat heal my tight muscles.

Lucky bastard. *Evil* bastard, I correct.

My lashes flutter as a yawn starts to rise up me, all the way from my belly to my jaw. I arch my back (crackles rain down it) and let my yawn loose.

The sound stirs Spike who, apparently, was also sleeping.

I turn onto my side, my back to him, wishing for slumber to find me once again. But I don't get the chance to slip back into that place of utter relaxation because something brushes over the warm skin of my thigh.

Spider!

I jolt upright, my wide, terrified gaze cutting down to my leg, just below the hemline of my dress. But ... that's no spider slinking over my skin. It's fingers.

I jerk back my leg and, in a blink, I've swivelled around to face Spike.

He gives me a sheepish look. "When will either of us get the chance again?" he tries to reason, but it only lifts rage to my heart and grips it in flames of its own.

I rip the strip from my mouth. "Don't fucking touch me," I seethe.

He sighs. "Come on," he croons. "It's not like we know we'll both survive this."

Then he does it.

He reaches out for my leg, his fingertips disappearing under the hem, and I react the best way I know how.

Both of my boots come flying out. And they both crack him hard on the face. I see the spray of blood before I hear the crunch of bone. The force of the kicks send him flying back, as far as his rope will allow.

I catch a fleeting glimpse of his face as he falls back. His nose is one smooshed, bloody mess and I know I've broken it. Not sorry.

Smacking down, he goes limp on the floorboards, his eyes fluttering for a beat before they shut entirely. He's been knocked out, and I hope he stays that way.

Good thing I know how to handle myself. All those years at a co-ed boarding school will instil those skills in just about anyone.

I knew it in my gut that I was right about him.

Who does that anymore? I mean, I can't guess the year we're in now, but the last one we left the world in, it was made pretty damn clear *not to touch women without their consent.* How hard is that to get through even the thickest of skulls?

I manage it every day of my life just fine.

I push out a huff, then turn to lean back against the pillar. At least now I have more space to stretch out (within the confines of the rope, of course).

And without the dark fae warrior and Spike around to prickle me with fear, I find that I sleep easily and deeply.

*

Heat burns my cheeks.

I flick my gaze to the floor as the warrior comes down the stairs wearing nothing but a black towel fastened low on his hips. His hips are widely built with muscle that the towel looks just about ready to slip off him and land on the hard oak steps.

Listening to the soft—almost inaudible—sound of his bare feet pad against the steps, I keep my gaze down on the toggle-rug in front of me.

Fear swells up in my throat; I swallow it back down. But that doesn't stop the panic from lifting up to envelope my chest.

He's at the bottom of the staircase now, turning into the open plan living space, and in mere heartbeats, he's going to see what I've done. His sharp eyes won't miss the knocked-out and bloody-faced Spike crumpled on the floor like a discarded, wrinkled ball of paper.

The fae moves silently now, even-footed and balanced. Still, his giveaway is the creak of a floorboard as he slips into the lounge.

My lips thin on the choppy breaths that threaten to break out of me.

Don't look up, don't look up.

If I don't look, he doesn't exist, and I won't face any punishment for attacking his other prisoner...right?

No such luck.

My whole body cringes as tanned legs step into my line of sight.

A frown pinches my brow at just how hairless his muscular legs are—as though every whisper of hair has been plucked out from his skin. But of course, I doubt a warrior like himself worries too much about body-hair grooming. He worries about how much blood he can shed in a day.

Reluctance bites at me as I lift my gaze up, along his damp, glistening body. I pass over the black fluffy towel, barely cinched at his hips, then up along his rippled chest where droplets of water drizzle over the defined lines—my cheeks grow hotter—to his stony face.

He stares down at me with total tedium in his near-black eyes. Those flecks of amber refuse to dance in the firelight coming from the hearth.

In his arm, he holds a bundle of leather armour against his injured side, so I can't see how well he's healed since the black powder back in the shed. But since he didn't spare any of that powder on his bullet wounds and they are vanished into kisses of purple bruises, I assume he's about healed now.

With a slight, nearly indecipherable shake of his head, he turns his muscular back on me and tosses his armour onto the leather couch. The landing topples over a throw-cushion.

He makes his way to the fire—and just stands there. He lets the heat dry him off; no use for a towel, I guess, other than to shield himself from me.

Are there customs like that in his world? Not to expose oneself when a woman is present, even if that woman is human?

The thought baffles me. All the possibilities and chances of what their cultures are like. I can barely understand some of those in my own world (well, the lost one), never mind from a different world altogether.

Keeping his scarred, glittering back to me, the warrior cuts into my thoughts as he stares into the fire and asks in a deep, growly voice, "Why?"

I blink, tearing my gaze from the dimples at the small of his back.

Why?

Why *what*?

It takes me a moment to realise what he means— Spike, unconsciousness, face covered in blood, a definitely broken nose.

Oh. That.

"He touched me," is all I say with a shrug that springs aches all over my shoulders and up my neck. I stretch out my back in response.

Silence comes. Maybe he's surprised that someone like me can stick up for herself; someone who vomits at the smell of charred skin and spews when cleaning bullet wounds, but has no problem breaking noses.

I learned my fighting, defensive skills at boarding school. Too many rich boys thinking they can get what they want and mummy and daddy will cover it up.

The only time I ever froze was with him—the warrior, when he cut open my bodice and pulled down my bra. That was terror of the iciest kind. That was a bone-deep, gut-churning fear of him and what he is, and knowing that I couldn't fight my way out of it if that's what he intended on doing.

Lucky me, he wants no such thing.

But if he's confused about my swinging violence and aversion, he best join the club. Not many people understand me. I have a hard enough time doing that myself. All I've come to recognise is that I'm a bit of a contradiction. But aren't we all in some way or another?

The fae has no answer. He continues watching the flames for a while, long after he's dry. And, Mother Earth help me, I can't *not* watch him.

Though the dark fae do not come from Earth, there is undeniably something earthly about them. Or about this one at least.

Those blackened ribbed scars give me a tingling feeling that I only get when I hold a new, fresh crystal in my palm. It shudders me with the power of nature and the earth. His skin is pulled so tight over his muscles that it almost seems as though he was born to look this way, born to become what he is—a warrior of the world, perhaps.

My mind is wandering to dangerous, ridiculous places. I stamp it out, fast.

Finally, he pulls away from the fire, and that helps my thoughts shift back to reality. But then he tugs the towel with the faintest of touches and it falls to the floor. He steps over it for his armour.

I should look away. But I have to see that bomb-wound.

I scan his side as he reaches for his leather trousers, and all I can see is the faintest whisper of a line. Not even a scar to be left behind—that line will probably heal too.

Unashamedly, I watch him tug on his armour pants, and I note with hot cheeks that he has a very nice bum. Really, is it all the hard training and muscle work to become a warrior that makes them all look as though they've been carved from marble? Or are they just … that way naturally?

Wearing only the trousers, he leaves the weapons belt, boots, and strappy chest armour on the couch when he turns to me.

In two strides, he's standing in front of me. I lean back as he reaches for my bound wrists. Gentler this time, he unravels the bindings until they ribbon off my skin.

Freed, I rub my bruises and wince.

Is he going to let me bathe?

Hope rises up in my chest—and it's quickly killed.

"Prepare meals," he commands, his voice a low growl.

My brows knit together. With a slanted mouth, I sputter, "You—you want me to … *cook?*"

Feminist rage swirls around me like a tornado out of nowhere.

"I'm not your housewife," I snarl at him with bravery fuelled solely by anger.

He cuts his gaze to the knocked-out Spike before sliding his eyes back to me, his lashes low.

"Your gender is unimportant to me," he tells me darkly. "But the moment you stop being useful is the moment I kill you." Slowly, he crouches down in front of me, resting his forearms on his knees. He leans in closer, shadows dancing over his dangerous-looking face. "Unlike my brethren, I see little advantage in saving your kind."

I pale, suddenly all too aware of the complete indifference he has towards us shifting into something worse—disdain.

Uncomfortable, I shift against the pillar. I look up at him from beneath my lashes and, when I ask, my voice is small; "Can I use the toilet first?"

He has little choice—it's either that or I'll go all over this floor.

7

I'm not exactly bursting for the loo, but I do have to *go*—if you know what I mean. Pee is not the urgency here.

So when the warrior takes me upstairs to the bathroom (connected to the toilet and bidet) and he just ... stands there at the door, I'm floored.

Cheeks getting hotter, I hover by the toilet in the corner of the tiled bathroom and blink at him. Like, get lost, all right? This shit is private!

He stares back at me and, in answer to my blank look, he folds his bare arms over his chest, then leans against the doorframe.

Flames roar up my hot-red face. Can't help but wiggle my hips a little, as though it will somehow help to keep everything in. But it's one of those cases where you get close to a toilet, and suddenly you just can't hold it anymore.

"Close the door," I murmur, doing my little shimmy dance.

A half-smile twists his mouth. He steps into the large bathroom then—kicks his foot back, slamming the door shut behind him. In his hand, he holds the lantern that he fished out of his satchel; it's pearlescent white flame lights up the bathroom like a ghost.

A flurry of annoyance tickles my chest.

I inhale deeply through my flaring nostrils.

"I need to be alone," I try again, lowering my gaze to the white-grouted tiles. This place was well cared for before the end. Maybe even after it, since it still seems to be in sharp shape, and there's little dust coating the tiles.

"I provide what you need," he warns, his tone dark enough to draw in my reluctant gaze. "Anything else is a luxury. I would deny you even this," he adds, lowering his long, thick lashes and tilting his chin down, "if the smell would not bother me."

Ok, I have a little tantrum of sorts. My arms throw down to my sides and I shake my hands and shudder my body with a petulant groan.

Can't be helped. I really need to fucking go. What's worse? Doing it in front of him or in my dress downstairs?

I know the better option is this one. So, with a huff, I reach under my dress, roll down my undies, and plonk down on the toilet seat.

Then performance-anxiety hits me, hard.

I look up at the ceiling, glance at the tub in the middle of the bathroom, assess the copper taps in the round sink. Nothing happens; my body, no matter how much it needs to, refuses me.

"Can you at least turn around?" I ask, cutting my gaze to him.

He wears an amused smirk on his face; a crack in the stone mask he normally wears. But at least he grants me this. He turns around and leans against the wall, a breath's touch away from the door.

With his back to me, I lean over to the sink and turn on the tap. The rush of water helps and he doesn't turn to berate me for it.

It flows easier now.

One of the best purposes of a dress. In a group, I could just squat down in the shadows and darkness and do my business.

Once I'm finished up, I flush then shift onto the bidet. Oh how I miss running water. And the tub—the tub!—is full of warm water. I can feel the gentle tendrils of heat roll out from the murky soap-filmed surface.

Eyeing the tub, I rinse my hands in the sink.

"I need to wash, too," I tell him, drying my hands on a small, soft towel.

I hear a scoff. He turns around, leans against the door, and crosses his arms. There's a ripple down his bicep.

"No." His answer is firm, unyielding.

I lower my lashes on him, eyes narrowed, and I step closer to the tub. Tossing the towel onto its edge, I hold his stare.

"I need the warm water for the aches in my body—the aches you gave me," I say, my voice rising with the flutter of anger in my chest. "You made me clean your wounds. I did that." *Sort of.* "So fucking excuse me for insisting on this one small thing."

I stink. I hurt. I ache. And I want that bloody bath.

His mouth tugs up at the corner. "Try it."

For a moment, we're at check. We stare at each other, both motionless and quiet, waiting for the other to move first.

It's me. I reach down for the zipper on the inside of my boot. And I barely grip it before large hands snatch my shoulders and I'm spun around.

A grunt catches in my throat as I'm slammed up against a wall.

The pressure shifts to my underarms and hoists me up.

My boots dangle above the tiles. He's so close to me that my nose grazes against his. I can taste the fresh toothpaste on his breath.

"Next time," he warns darkly, "I'll take those photographs from your boot." He leans closer, his lips tingling against mine. I hitch my breath. "And with them, I will deliver one hundred cuts to your flesh. *Then* you may complain about pain."

The pressure releases and I land on my boots, upright. Aches shoot up my spine like long needles.

A grimace hides my wince. The threat he delivered is what tightens my chest most.

The dark fae snatches my upper-arm and drags me out of the bathroom. He hauls me down the stairs at a pace too quick, and I stumble and stagger beside him.

When we reach the pillar, I see that Spike is awake. Well, sort of. His lashes hang so low that if they didn't flutter, I would think he was still asleep.

But I don't go to the post to join the dazed Spike.

The dark fae steers me into the open kitchen, only releasing me when I stumble into the island bench. He's about to leave before he pauses to run me over with a narrowed, dark look, then cuts his gaze to the backdoor.

I trace his stare. But before I can even think about any possible escape plan, he's got the fridge in his grip and starts pushing it to the door, as though it's nothing but a coffee table.

He blocks the door.

Before he makes to pass by me, he studies my pinched face. "Is there an issue?" he asks, arching his brow.

Looking down at the scuffed toes of my boots, I shrug one shoulder. "I don't know how to cook."

Sort of.

It's not like I haven't helped along the way when I could to learn, in case I ever ended up on my own. But I burn a lot of stuff, so my practice was limited by the others in the group.

The dark fae gives me a dark look.

My hands find each other at my front. Fingers fidgeting, I explain, "I had people always do it for me."

I feel his watchful eyes on me.

And then he leaves me to cook for him like a fucking servant.

8

Call me a hopeful idiot, but I'm making *a lot* of spaghetti and pasta sauce. There's quite a supply in the pantries and since the gas still works on the stove, I have no problems boiling the water.

As I set the saucepan on the burner, I glance back at the lounge.

The dark fae has his back to me. He's rubbing a balm over his almost-totally-healed wounds. The firelight flickers over his muscles, giving the illusion that they ripple. He throws no looks over his shoulder at me—no telling me off for my over-the-top pasta estimations.

I made enough for all three of us, two servings.

Spike is still slumped against the pillar at a twisted angle, but I squint at his profile and see (with the help of the firelight) that his hooded eyes are open. So he'll be awake for meal-time. If he can stomach what *I* make, that is.

At the bubbling sound of a pot boiling over, I rush back to the stove. Water foams all over, but all I do is turn down the burner a tad then give the spaghetti a stir. Not my kitchen, so there's little use in cleaning down the cooktop.

Another look back at the lounge.

Spike is still in place.

With a damp cloth, the dark fae cleans his leathered armour clothes.

And I'm left feeling like a fucking maid as I set out bowls on the island bench. My hands are clammy from all the steam off the pot; a bowl slips from my grip and crashes to the floor. It shatters at the toes of my boots—

I feel the tension suffocate the air.

I stiffen, looking up at the lounge.

Spike has twisted all the way around, his wide and puffy eyes on me, filled with terror. And the dark fae has risen from the couch, wandering his way towards me.

My gaze swerves to his hand. Loose in his grip, he carries a small knife.

As he steps into the kitchen, his eyes do a quick sweep of the space before he advances on me, moving like a panther around the island bench.

He looks down at the tiles.

I'm frozen by the sudden terror in the air; radiating from Spike. I can't look anywhere but at the dark fae's stone-cold face.

He studies the shattered bowl hugged around my boots for a heartbeat. When he finally lifts his gaze to mine, a tedious frown pinches his brows together.

"Be quiet," he says then walks out, back to the couch.

Uh...

Well I was expecting a bit more than that.

I'm not 'disappointed' of course, but by the way Spike was acting and looking at me, I definitely was expecting a beating or something. It's a relief that he left me alone, but really ... *why* did he?

Is he just one of the nicer dark fae warriors out there?

My forehead creases as I turn my perplexed stare on Spike. He looks just as baffled as I feel and, after a moment in which he seems to forget all about my breaking his nose, he just shrugs and turns back around.

I've heard stories of the dark fae from Spike. Stories that they have stripped skin from bone for a kuri simply over brewing their earthy coffees or failing to pitch their tents on time, or one time—for refusing to dance for them.

So how did I get away without a scratch?

Then it dawns on me. *Be quiet*, he told me.

He doesn't want anyone to know we are here. Any nearby survivors could be alerted to our presence—*his* presence. After our bombing, he must know by now that to some of our groups, he is vulnerable, all alone with two kuris who would turn against him in a heartbeat.

So be quiet it is—for now. Because I don't need another group coming to my rescue. I only need time and a plan to do what I promised I would.

Kill the warrior.

Plates are balanced on my spread-out hands and another is tucked in the edge of my bent elbow. Never done this before—balanced so many plates and forks—but I've seen plenty of servers and waitresses do it, so ... that's practically the same thing, right?

Apparently not; I rattle louder than I walk.

The dark fae looks up from his weapons belt—he's polishing the blades—as I come in. For a beat, he glances at the three very full plates of pasta and sauce. But he cares little about my making meals for both me and Spike, too.

He goes back to his dagger, the same one he plunged into the corpses back at the village.

I take the plates over to him first and I wait. He might like to choose which one he wants. But he spares no more looks my way, so I crouch and slip a plate from my palm onto the coffee table before joining Spike at the pillar.

Sliding down the pillar, I hand him a plate.

His scowl furrows deep into his skin, ageing him a decade. Fury ignites his ordinary brown eyes into pits of shimmering mud. Oh, he wants revenge for me busting up his nose.

Still, he takes the plate, his bound hands clenched so tightly that they make me think of claws. Just by looking at his tense, crooked fingers, I can feel his aches in my own.

Hesitantly, I wrap pasta around my fork then lift it to my mouth. I cast a glance at the warrior. He's turned all the way around to lean against the spine of the couch. Ignoring the cutlery, he eats with his fingers, staining his fingertips blood-red (I might have added a half-bottle of red wine to the sauce, but when and where you can, right?)

In silence we eat.

Both Spike and I stay tucked over ourselves. The fear of having our meals snatched away is dug into our hunched shoulders and curved backs.

The warrior seems to have entirely forgotten about us, though. He watches the flames in the hearth, his eyes glistening like liquid fire, and his mind far away from this moment in time.

Still, despite his distraction, I eat too fast. And I end up with a tummy ache by the time I'm licking my plate clean.

With a groan, I slide my plate from my lap to the floor. Reclining against the pillar, my hands find my bloated belly and rub, and I browse my gaze around the lounge.

The only welcoming feature of this space is the white-painted bookshelf against the wall, at the corner of the seat window. Oh, I'd love to snatch a book from there, spread out on the window-seat, and bask in the sun.

The sun.

Shit, I miss it. I miss the sunshine warming my skin and lightening my hair and drawing out beads of sweat down my spine. All of it; the pleasant and the unpleasant.

What I would give for one more day with a bright, hot sky glaring down at me.

And what I would do for one of those books on that floor-to-ceiling shelf. Even with the firelight, it's hard to make out the dusty titles, but I do recognise a spine here and there.

'Breakfast at Tiffany's' stands out to me. One of my favourites from school, learning all about the coded messages in the book for the gay underground back in those days.

Capote was a brave bastard. I still can't believe this book of his isn't in the literary canon. That shit needs to be branded a classic.

Total dejection suddenly crushes me like a rainfall of stones.

I'll never read another book, another classic. I'll never discuss the suspected homophobia of Bloom—and thus, the rejection of Capote's 'Breakfast at Tiffany's' from the canon—with anyone ever again.

I'll never discuss the perfect lighting for photographs, the classic cameras, how difficult it is to capture the perfect moon on the perfect night.

All those people with the same interests as me—dead.

All those people still surviving around me—dangerous and completely uncultured and uneducated in this world ... Just as I would be in the dark realm, if I was ever unfortunate enough to get there.

In fact, that's something I make note of to ask Spike later. Are the dark fae armies carting bands of kuris simply for slavery in this world or ... do they intend to make them slaves in *their* world?

That thought terrifies me. It floods me with ice-cold spears through my body until I press back against the pillar and bring my knees to my chest.

I swallow, hard.

Need to kill him before he kills me or worse, take me back to his world.

But—

Fuck!

I had the chance.

I had the chance and I missed it completely!

I made his damn dinner—a direct passage way between potential poison and his insides. A perfect way to commit murder ... for me anyway. Not about the blood and gore, but I can deal with some vomit.

Next time.

And there will be a next time, because he trusts me to make his dinner now. He sets the plate down on the coffee table, then leans back to rest for a bit, shutting his eyes.

Ok, so maybe I missed my first shot, but that doesn't make a loss. No failures, only lessons learned, right?

The lesson I learned?

Poison the shit out of his next meal.

Hopefully that comes sooner than later. Because right now, I'm suffering. Not only do I have the worst spot at the pillar (a little too away from the heat of the fireplace for my liking) and I have this ghastly swelling in my tummy (note to self; don't overload on carbs when you've been starving for weeks), I have to stare at that fucking bookshelf.

I have counted a few more in my quiet, sullen moment.

'Jane Eyre'; 'Sense and Sensibility'; 'Catcher in the Rye'; 'Twilight' (what an odd addition to the collection).

My faraway book thoughts are shattered as the warrior suddenly pushes up from the couch. My eyelids are heavy and tired as I look up at him.

He advances on me, the same food-coma pulling at his eyelids. Then I realise, as he reaches down for my rope, that he needs to secure me to the pillar before taking rest.

I blink, surprised, as he tugs the rope, guiding me to stand. I get to my feet, balance swaying, hands still pressed firm against my belly.

Peppermint tea, I would order if I were at home in my villa.

He guides me over to the couch and the frown in my forehead deepens with each step. Face like a crumpled hand-towel, I watch as he scoops his free hand under the couch and—easily—lifts it up. He hooks my rope around the leg of the couch once, thrice, around and around until he fastens it into a knot that I don't recognise.

I only know sailing knots, but this one is ... complicated. Maybe from his world, not mine.

Either way, when he lets the couch thud back into place, I hear just how heavy it is, and I know there's no way I can lift my way out of this restraint.

He flops down on the couch. It creaks under his weight as he turns his back to the fire and gets himself comfortable.

I throw a look back at Spike. Hard to tell with his busted nose and all, but he looks like he's scowling at me. Confused or furious, I don't know.

It isn't lost on me that I got the better position here. I'm directly across from the fire, I have the couch to lean against and the fluffy rug to lie down on.

The pull of my full stomach can't be fought for long. Soon, I can't keep my eyes open or stifle the yawns stretching through my jaw.

I lean on my side, curl up, and shut my eyes.

Food coma gets its hooks deep in me.

9

"She's killed people before. She's dangerous."

Those hushed words snare into my dreams.

Where a woman howls in agony, cradling her lover's head on her lap, her cries are those viciously spoken words. Her grey hair falls down the side of her face like a veil to the afterlife, and she just howls and cries, tears running down her wrinkled face.

She looks so oddly familiar with those faint freckles on her cheeks and her ocean-blue eyes wet with tears.

Turning my back on her and all her pain, I see that we are in the middle of a cobblestone street. Not one I particularly recognise, since they all start to look the same after some time. And the houses here are faceless; no doors or windows or even any roofs.

Feels like I'm not supposed to be here.

It's too ... *quiet.*

That's when I notice the thickness, the *pressure*, of the silence.

I look back at her; the woman stops screaming. She stares right at me, no more lover's head on her lap, no more tears streaking down her face.

Her expression is slack, almost stunned. I blink once before I see it. The growth of crimson on her chest and—the wink of a dagger glinting out from between her ribs.

Her thinned lips move. She speaks out the corner of her mouth, "She will kill you, I promise that. Can't you see how violent she is? I've seen her disembowel your kind before."

I cock my head to the side, a curious frown wrinkling my face. Her voice is deepening into something male, but weak and slimy.

I watch the older woman as she goes on, "The bomb was her idea."

"Why are you lying?" I ask, an innocent and curious touch to my soft voice. Dream has its hooks in me.

In answer, she bows over herself, her shaky hands come to the crimson pool at her middle. The dagger is gone, no more winks or glares. And darkness starts to seep in from the edges of the street.

"Open your eyes," the woman whispers, her voice gentle suddenly, so unlike the male tone she wore before.

And those are her final words before I'm plunged into the familiar thick black. I stand alone in nothingness, blinking and blinking, trying to wake myself up.

As dreams start to slip away to reality, I begin to feel the plush touch of the rug against my side, my stiff and aching body curled up into a ball—

And I hear the familiar male's voice speak in a whisper; "If you don't get rid of her now, you will be next. I mean only to serve you, master."

Spike.

Fucking Spike, selling me out to the devil.

It all locks in place, puzzle pieces coming together after a fog. He wants revenge for my self-defence, the slime ball.

Before I can open my eyes and defend myself again, the couch creaks near my head.

There's a shuffle. The sound of feet on the floor, muffled by a rug. Air disturbs all around me, and I get the sense that the dark fae is walking past me on the floor.

Peering out of one eye, I watch through the daze of sleep glossing over my sight. The warrior strides towards Spike, still tethered to the pillar.

Spike recoils from him, a wince twisting his face. But all the warrior does is touch his fingertips to his neck—then Spike gapes up at him, his mouth opening and closing like a stunned goldfish.

He can't talk.

I'm yanked back to a moment in time when something of the same sorts happened to me. The dark fae had me on the ground, cornered and defeated, and no matter how much I tried, I couldn't cry out the pain he inflicted on me. I couldn't so much as make a squeak.

So he really does have a power to silence us.

Fleetingly, I wonder if this power extends to the other fae as well, or just him. Are they unique in this way? A specific, special ability for each of them? Or is it a trick of the fae that they all share?

Those thoughts need a good slapping out of my mind.

I don't need to understand my enemies to kill them. And really, I only need to kill one. Among all the lies that Spike told, he was right about one thing—I *will* kill this warrior.

Just give me the chance ... again.

I wait a long while before I realise the dark fae hasn't come back to the couch. His near-silent footsteps pad to the corner of the room, where I think the bookshelf is (my hearing got a whole lot better after being in the dark for so long).

Finally, I take the chance and pretend to have just woken up. I start with a dazed blink, the kind that comes after a thick and heavy dream. Then a natural yawn stretches my jaw and with it, I push out my arms and legs, feeling that euphoric sensation ripple through me.

The sigh of pleasure that escapes me draws in *his* attention.

He's moved to the fireplace, holding stacks of books in his hands, and he watches me over his shoulder. Long, thick lashes hang low over ember eyes; his jaw is clenched tight, indents marking the space between jawline and cheek.

He looks away first, tugging his attention back to the fireplace.

Then my heart thrashes in my chest as he tosses the piles of books into the fireplace.

"No!" I cry out, kicking the blanket off my legs (when the hell did I get a blanket?). "No, you can't do that!"

Bare back to me, he simply responds, "Words are fuel."

Words are fuel?

What the fuckery does that mean and how does it give him the right to burn our books—our histories and cultures?

Well, it's not like that isn't an obvious part of their mission, to destroy all that we have ever created. But still, watching him toss those precious, beautiful bound lumps of paper and words and blood, sweat and tears into a roaring fire just kills me inside.

Something inside of me bursts open, red hot flames flooding me.

I scramble towards him as fast as I can. I make it halfway across the rug before the rope (I forgot about that) yanks me back.

This catches his attention. With only a few books left in his hands, he turns all the way around to look down at me. For a moment, he watches me frantically pull against the rope. It's no use.

Purposefully, he stretches out one hand—one book—and drops it. It thuds to the rug within arm's reach of me.

'Little Women'.

A gasp catches in my throat, one of hunger, and I propel myself forward. Just as my hand slaps down on the cover, a bare foot comes crashing down on my palm.

My cry is muffled by gritted teeth. Seething, I glower up at him, my chest heaving with breaths of rage.

He's baiting me, the sick fuck. Punishing me still for shooting him.

The pressure increases; my bones crackle and my muffled gritting sound swells into an outright shout.

"What would you give for it?" He taunts me with his light tone and wicked smirk and dancing-amber eyes. "A finger? A whole hand?"

Your life.

Those words sting my tongue. But I'm smarter than that.

Bide my time to take us both out. An obviously better option than just feeding into Spike's planted seeds of doubt and having him kill me right here and now.

Looking up at him from beneath my lashes, I hiss, "What do you want?"

His face falls for a beat; shuttering. In a blink, it's turned to stone and he stares down at me like a statue in Rome, utterly impassive.

"From you," he says darkly, "nothing."

Lifting his foot, he releases my hand. I jerk it back and hold it to my chest, fingers massaging out the aches and pains buried deep in my bones.

Before I can flick my attention back to 'Little Women', he's snatched it up. He tosses it into the flames to be devoured and destroyed.

Eyes on me, he adds, "You have enough on your person." And he cuts a look to my boot, where the photographs are tucked away.

I swallow back a lump in my throat.

I lose the stand-off and slink back to the couch. As I lean against its base, I slide a glower to Spike. He watches me with narrowed eyes, his bruised lip lifting at the bow into an ugly snarl.

In answer, I flip him off.

Try me, bitch.

But no one tries me for the rest of the hour, and beyond. I'm left to wallow in my pit of misery as the fae burns every single book in the lounge. When he's done casually destroying a full collection of human history and culture, he fishes out a folded parchment sheet and a charcoal stick from a satchel, then spreads it over the coffee table.

A map.

I lean closer, my chin lifted to better look down at it. He makes no effort to hide it from my prying eyes either. It's as though I suddenly don't exist anymore.

Using the charcoal stick, he amends an already-there line around the map. And I recognise it all; what the map is, what he is doing. It's the path of his unit—and he's rerouting his way around the villages and farms to meet his comrades. He finishes by drawing an X at the end of a landmass—France's coast.

By leaning a little closer and squinting my eyes, I can faintly make out where the X is. Around Calais. Near the English Channel Tunnel.

That's where he plans to link with his unit (whose path on the map curves all the way around the coast). He'll make it in time, since he's redrawn his own path in a straight diagonal line, cutting off most of the villages and towns between us and his unit.

My mind whirls with times and hours and days, but I can't make sense of any of it anymore. Somewhere around a week is what I would guess for us to make it to the Tunnel. A few days longer for his army since they have to stop and burn towns along the way.

Before I can study the map a second longer, I'm suddenly thrown back. The warrior shoved me hard between the breasts, and I slam back against the couch.

He glares at me and my response is a glower of my own.

Shaking his head, he packs up the map. He's buckling the satchel when I feel the weight in my belly and bladder.

"I need the loo," I tell him.

Tensions stiffens him for a beat. He's hunched over the satchel, his head bowed and, after a heartbeat, he lifts his dark gaze to mine. There's a warning in there somewhere, but I find I don't quite care when my body is starting to writhe for release.

"Weak human," he mutters before he pushes up from the floor, kicks the satchel to the side, then reaches down for me. As he unties me from the couch's leg, he murmurs more insults in his own language (sounds like barbed wire to my ears).

Out the corner of my eye, I catch Spike's lips moving. He looks to be shouting at us, his mouth forming readable words 'Me too!', but I just smirk at him still under the silence-spell, and look away.

I told you to try me.

The warrior makes no effort to hide his hard expression or sigh of annoyance as he takes me upstairs, his hand firm around my bony bicep, his other grip loose on the lantern.

A bit too chirpy at getting under his skin, I tell him, "Think happy thoughts. Think about the smells you're avoiding."

"Be silent." His tone is firm and gravelly, reminding me all over again of barbed wire.

"Make me," I mutter, and I know he can.

But he doesn't.

He just shoves me into the bathroom (the tub is still full of water, calling out to me) and gestures to the toilet in the corner.

It hasn't gotten any easier the second time around. My cheeks still burn with the flames of fire as I empty myself. And I avoid his gaze the whole time, knowing full well that he's watching me too closely.

When I use the bidet to clean my bits, I glance up at him, keeping the dress down far enough to shield myself. There's a trace of a frown on his forehead, his mouth turned down at the corner, and he studies me as though I am some sort of puzzle to be worked out.

Maybe fae don't need the loo as much as we do, and that baffles him?

I chance my luck when I'm done and wash my hands in the sink. Glancing at him in the mirror, I see that he still watches me—but his eyes are faraway and glazed, and he doesn't really see me. I risk it and use soapy hands to wash my face.

He doesn't stop me.

A part of me itches to riffle through the cabinets and drawers and see what else I can get away with. But I think I've pushed my luck far enough today, so I dab my face dry on a towel, then wander over to him.

He blinks out of his thoughts, his gaze landing on me. He watches me for a beat before he kicks away from the doorframe, then leads the way out of the bathroom. This time, he doesn't hold onto my arm with the strength of a boulder crushing bone.

I follow behind him.

And this newfound trust he has of me doesn't go unnoticed; it works quite well with my plans of poisoning him.

10

It truly seemed like we were going to move on from this house sometime this day (or night, or whatever), but he settles in on the couch, legs spread out, hands tucked behind his head and stares at the chandelier on the ceiling.

The dark fae's wounds look completely healed, his strength has returned tenfold. The only thing that would slow us down now would be me and my injuries.

Unfortunately for me, I don't have any magical powders to treat the bruises littering me or the blood-clotted gash at the back of my head.

But of course I'm not foolish enough to think he's hanging back here for my benefit. Why would he?

No, he's waiting for something else. Maybe he senses more survivors in the area, and means to avoid them. Maybe he knows he has more leisurely time for rest with his new route to meet up with his unit.

I don't pretend to know the workings of a dark fae warrior's mind, but I'd bet my left leg it's all fucked up in there. And that's my strong leg—the one I best used in ballet and figure skating back in the day.

Fuck, I miss those days.

I dodged most of university classes for those hobbies.

That's what my mother called them anyway. *Hobbies.* But to me, like my terrible photography, it was just a part of who I am—*was.* There is no ballet or figure skating anymore. There is no part of any of that still within me, other than hollow yearning.

At least I have the photographs.

At the bottom of the couch, I slip the pictures out from my boot and study them in the strong firelight.

By the pillar, Spike still squirms and mouths for the loo, but he goes ignored. Don't know why the dark fae forgets about him. It's not like Spike is any worse than I am to the warrior. Surely we are the same to him, equally as despicable and ... gross?

Now that I think about it, what does he see when he looks at us? How do the dark fae see us not as a whole species, but as individuals? I wonder if they even have the compassionate capacity to see beyond their missions.

Probably not. I make my decision on it firmly when a bare foot nudges the small between my shoulder blades.

I throw a dark look over at the warrior, sprawled out over the couch.

"Meal," he demands, then looks back up at the ceiling.

My mouth puckers in annoyance, and I stuff the photos back into my boot. Not sure I'm cut out for slavery.

But...

Buuuut!!

This is it. The chance I've been waiting for—the chance to poison this demon. And instantly, cold fear floods my belly and I have the urge to use the loo again.

Still, I force myself up from the couch (he hasn't tethered me back since the toilet) and straighten out the skirt of my dress. It's all crumpled from the blanket that falls to the floor.

"Take him," the dark fae adds.

A frown tugs my brows together.

My pout puckers even more and I slide my stare to Spike.

Going to be a lot harder to poison the fae while Spike is in the kitchen with me. I study him for a beat, my mind spinning.

Somehow, he's managed to hold his toilet urges, but I see the hope light up his eyes. And I can use that.

"Fine."

I march over to him and untie him from the pillar (it takes a solid five minutes, and I've worked on plenty of sailor's knots before). His silence still swallows him whole, so for the moment, I say nothing about his need for the loo.

I wander into the kitchen, Spike at my heels, his body clenched tight. He stands in the middle of the room, away from me thankfully, and watches as I start to rummage through the cupboards and pantries.

Don't want pasta again since there's a bit more variety than what I've been used to these past twenty months (that's my guess, at least). Now, I have options—and what a delight to be able to choose my final meal.

So I make it a good one.

Ordering Spike around (fill that pot with water, boil that, cut these), I unload my loot on the island bench: tinned asparagus, a bottle of lemon juice, canned peaches for dessert (my dessert, at least), ham-flavoured baked beans, rice and soy sauce, and finally the one that matters, the one that I can stir the poison into, pumpkin soup.

Quite the spread. A lethal one.

And it's now that I study my loot that I make my decision. I should poison the life out of Spike, too.

Yet that risks my plan.

You see, I need him to use the toilet. To poison the food, he needs to be in the loo and so does the warrior. After that, it still works for me, because if the warrior survives the poisoning somehow, I need Spike to take the fall. We will play the blame game, and I have a feeling I'm the one with the most trust here. But then, all those threats I made might fall back to the opposite of my favour.

Ahhh, it's so risky. All of it. But I'm determined, and as I start pulling out plates and bowls, I shout out to the dark fae that Spike is about to wet himself. To better my plan, I add that it's unhygienic around the food.

There's a gruff groan from the lounge before he appears at the archway and summons Spike over.

I get to work as soon as I hear them head halfway up the stairs.

Under the sink is my first and only destination. Really, I was hoping for detergent or bleach, but what I find is much, much better than that.

Rat poison.

Ah, the countryside.

The warrior's ploy to take quiet roads and villages backfired.

I empty the box of powdered rat poison into the pumpkin soup. All of it, every last dusting of beige. Then I stir it in, fast, and shove the empty box to the back of the under-the-sink cupboard.

They return sooner than I expected. But I'm safe, just stirring the soup when Spike scurries into the kitchen.

Before the dark fae heads back to the lounge, I call out to him, "I need the loo again."

He throws me a withering look.

In answer, I shrug. "I think I'm about to bleed."

His eyes roll back for a fleeting moment. His exhaustion of me is palpable. Yet, he summons me over and leads me up to the bathroom for the second time that day—providing me with the alibi I need. Now, Spike is alone with the food, and I have plausible deniability.

I head straight for the cupboards and drawers. Inside, I find a half-empty pack of pads and one tampon. Not a woman's house, then. Or the residents took most of it when evacuations spread through the countryside.

To the vexation of the warrior, I take my damn time. Eventually—when I'm reading the trivia on the pad-wrapper (I love this brand)—he slides down the wall to sit on the floor, and just watches me.

Some of this trivia I've read before. It's my preferred brand for this very reason, I have reading material when I'm changing the bits. But today, I learn a new piece of utterly useless information.

"Did you know humans can't lick their elbows?" I ask, tossing the wrapper away. I ache to try it, but that's embarrassing, isn't it?

He says nothing.

I lean back against the basin and unravel the pad in my slender fingers. "Can your kind lick their elbows?"

His lashes lower. "I have never tried, nor heard of such nonsense before."

I hum. "If you can't do it, you could just say that."

His mouth twitches, fighting off a snarl.

Reaching under my dress, I slap the pad onto my undies (keeping my bits from his gaze—a gaze that flicks downwards), then fix them back up.

"Are there humans in your world?" I ask, kicking away from the sink.

He pushes up from the floor, his weary stare on me. I don't expect him to answer me but before I reach the door, he says, "Some."

I arch a pale eyebrow. "Slaves?"

"Among other things."

My lashes flutter with a startled blink. "Like ... what?" What could be worse than slaves?

He doesn't answer and instead, ushers me out of the bathroom.

On the way down, another thought pops into my mind and, really, what do I have to lose with our looming deaths?

"Is there any light in your world?"

Silence is my answer as we take the stairs. When we reach the bottom, he says, "The fruit shines, the grass gleams, and the roads glow."

My heart twists at the thought, pictures of what this fantasy land could look like swarming my mind.

Before I can settle on any one image, I see the coffee table—and the plates and three bowls on it, waiting for us.

My stomach flips with dread.

Spike sits cross-legged at the corner of the table, watching us with suspicion narrowing his eyes.

As far as I know, all three of those bowls are poisoned. But a new threat chills me—what if Spike had the same idea, and poisoned my food too?

I intend to die after the warrior does. But not before I have a wash in the tub and enjoy a cigarette from my shoulder bag and browse through the house, then maybe sit outside in the fresh air for a while.

I'd hoped to enjoy my last moments.

Now, I don't know if I'll get the chance.

II

Eyes on the plates, my steps slow as I move around the couch. Just as I come to the coffee table and make to crouch down, a sudden hand snatches the nape of my neck—and I'm yanked off my feet.

The warrior has grabbed and pulled me onto the couch.

I go sprawling over his lap, face-down on the leather. His hand still grips tight onto the nape of my neck, holding me down.

For a heartbeat, I'm utterly still. He knows. He knows, he knows, he knows. Somehow, he's learned what I did to the soup—and I'll be crushed for it.

But then...

A strange, itchy sensation tickles the back of my head.

Stunned, I blink as I figure out what the odd feeling is: He's peeling away strands of my hair from my head wound.

Total silence crushes the room, and that pressure keeps me down on his lap more than the grip on my neck. I'm motionless as he shifts away for a beat, then I hear rummaging as he fishes through a satchel.

Before my mind can click onto what he's doing to me, he's doing it—spreading a balm over my head wound. And that stings, I tell you.

Against the leather, my face twists with a grimace and I sink my fingers into the couch as far as they will go. A groan rumbles up me, but he keeps on dabbing his salved-fingertips over the gash.

Wonder what it looks like now. Still hurts like all hell, but how has the healing gone? Is it all congealed, crispy blood or a lumpy line of that glazed-like blood that reminds me of the inside of a jellybean?

For the dark fae warrior to decide to heal the wound, he must suspect it to be worse than *I* thought. Maybe he needs to get us moving on soon and he's concerned that the injury will slow us down.

Who knows why he does the things that he does. I sure as shit don't.

The pressure from my neck lifts and it's like a breath fills me out of nowhere, flooding me with relief and oxygen. With a lift of his thigh, he nudges me off of him.

I push up from his lap, avoiding his gaze, and slip down to the floor.

Spike's gaze burns hot into my red cheek.

There's no secret about it. I'm not the mule, my wounds are healed—though this could all be to avoid me slowing him down—and I slept on the rug with a blanket and in direct line to the fireplace. If the warrior has a favourite ... well, it's pretty damn obvious that it's me. But again, that's a big *if,* isn't it? Really, he's focusing his attention more on me so that I heal and recover better, and we can head on soon.

I slip a plate off of the coffee table.

Throwing a cautious glance at the dark fae, I check that it's all right to start eating. But he just shifts on the couch, watching me with that familiar frown between his brows. He rests his forearms on his thighs, hunches over a little, and considers me with firelight eyes, mirroring the flames in the hearth.

I clear my throat and look down at my plate of lemon-juiced asparagus.

Lifting a strip up by the stalk, I nibble on the grainy end, and that triggers Spike into eating too.

He pulls his plate onto his lap. And we eat in silence.

The warrior watches me for a while longer before he reaches for his food. My heart leaps into my throat as his hand cups the soup bowl.

He tucks in, finally yanking his frowny gaze away from me.

I chance a glance at Spike. His brows are all furrowed and bushy, and on his juice-stained lips (he must have been guzzling some orange juice in the kitchen while I was in the bathroom) he wears a grim look.

Suspicion has his eyes narrowed, and I know he is wondering why the hell the dark fae healed me.

In answer, I just shrug.

He shakes his head and scoops up a spoonful of beans.

I'm cautious about my meal. Asparagus seems the safest option, so I take my fine-ass time nibbling on them down to the final stalk. By then, the warrior has finished the last of his soup and he trades the bowl for the large plate of rice smothered in soy sauce.

He doesn't get a single mouthful of the rice before it happens.

The plate falls from his hand and thuds to the rug. Rice splatters.

I turn my widening eyes on him, my heart suddenly stopped in my chest. I swallow back a lump just as a wretched gurgling sound crawls up the warrior's throat and then—

Holy shit.

He heaves forward just as black blood comes flying out of his mouth.

Scrambling back from the spray, I drop my plate; lemon juice spills all over the floor. I kick off of the rug, another spray of thick black, unnatural blood spilling out all over the coffee table.

Spike just sits there, his eyes wide and mouth parted, and watches as the warrior shoves up from the couch and, crouched over, lets blood spill out of his mouth like a constant stream of water from a tap.

I can't stop it; a retch of my own throws my body forward. Didn't expect to see much blood—not this much at least. And now I've gone and triggered myself.

I turn over onto all fours and spew up the asparagus. The lemon juice burns my throat coming up. It's a vomity-bloody disaster in here.

The floor thuds beneath me as the warrior storms out of the lounge and into the kitchen. I glance up, tears in my eyes (why do I end up crying every time I vomit?), and see that he lets it all come out into the sink.

A shudder rinses my body. With a look back over my shoulder, I notice that Spike has stood up at some point and backed up to the wall, his wide eyes now on me.

He knows.

But he doesn't get the chance to accuse me—yet.

Storming back into the lounge, the warrior wears fiery eyes that light up the room, and a furious twist to his face. His eyes shift between Spike, huddled by the wall, and me, crouched on the floor with my own vomit on my hands.

I loosen a shuddering breath.

It didn't work. It was enough to hurt him, make him ill—but he's standing there, tall and strong, inde-fucking-structible.

Well, shit.

Guess I should have eaten the soup at the same time. I would have died before he got the chance to punish me.

But—I can't believe my luck when—he barges past me and heads straight for Spike.

Falling onto my bum, I turn and watch as Spike backs up into the bookshelf. It rattles as he lifts up his hands.

"It was her," he whispers, his voice trembling. "It wasn't me, I swear—I would never, I could ..."

His words fail him as the warrior stops in front of him. His back muscles are tense balls of lead with beige skin pulled tight over them.

Slowly, he looks over his shoulder at me. And the embers in his eyes burn through my soul.

I shake my head and point frantically at Spike. "It was him! I was with you in the bathroom!"

"So was I!" Spike shouts, so terrified that he jumps on the spot. "I told you she would do this," he adds, looking pleadingly at the fae, "I told you she would deliver on her promise. This is what she does, who she is."

The fae snatches Spike by the side of the neck, then hauls him over to me. He throws him down on the floor so hard that I hear his knees crack. Spike flips around, looking up at the fae—but his murderous eyes are for me, and only me.

"*I'll kill you the first chance I get,*" the warrior echoes words I once swore to him.

I pale, feeling the drain of blood plummet to my worrying gut. Numbly, I shake my head—but it's all I can muster, and it's not enough.

He reaches for me.

I scramble back, but I'm not fast enough. His hand snatches my neck up and, in a swift and strong tug, I'm lifted onto my feet and slammed back against the wall.

My grunt is muffled by the grip pressing against my throat.

The warrior brings his face to me, the tickle of his nose on mine itching me. "Tell me your name."

I blink, surprise slackening my face. His grip loosens just enough for me to croak out, "Coralie."

"*Cora-lee*," he parrots in his earthly accent, thick and barbed, "how I will make you suffer."

I see the wink of a dagger in his hand.

And I shut my eyes, tight.

Please, make it quick.

Please, kill me softly.

end of book 2
mind the cliff.

QUINN BLACKBIRD

PLEASE REVIEW ON AMAZON & GOODREADS

I love to read your feedback, thoughts, comments—or even just see a simple star rating.

I hope you enjoyed book two of Dark Fae: Extinction. Dark Fae: Extinction is the second series in the "Dark Fae" Universe, by Quinn Blackbird.

The Dark Fae series (first series) is available in box set and paperback format on my Amazon profile.

Please remember to review this book, I would absolutely adore to hear your thoughts and feedback, or even just to see a star-rating! Reviews are fuel to us authors—they help promote our work which, in turn, gives us more time and opportunities to continue what we do best ... produce more stories for you!

KEEP READING FOR A '*DARK FAE, BOOK 1* SAMPLE'

I hear him before I see him; the purposeful steps he takes up the alley, the clink of armour, the song of a dagger he sheathes.

I turn my head to the mouth of the alley, where the main street blazes orange. And I see his silhouette first. Tall, broad—consuming.

Danger creeps up my spine. I have the sudden urge to break free and run at the other dark fae. I don't want to face this one coming up the alley, the one all the others fall silent for.

My breath is deep and shaky as I see him completely engulfed in firelight.

The darkness fades from him, but lashes of it seem to lick at his heels, as though the darkness itself belongs to him, he is their master, their home. His soft-soled boots are thin, onyx-black leather, matching the trousers that grip him.

At his hips hangs a belt that's home to all kinds of daggers and throwing knives. Some blades wear traces of fresh blood, and my spine shivers at the sight of the crimson smears gleaming in firelight.

Chain-link armour—so fine that it appears to have been made from silk threads—clings to a black-leather vest he wears. Paler than moonlight, his skin is scarred all over. His arms, muscular and strong, are ribbed by these strange scars. They aren't bumped like the scars that scatter my arms, but pale and jagged not unlike stretch marks. They climb up his neck like claws, and stop just before the strong jawline.

His face steals me.

I've seen some dark fae from a distance before, and up close and personal today. They are all beautiful in the most dangerous of ways, like deadly cobras or lethal panthers. But this one… he's something else.

His sleek dark hair falls to the side and brushes over his raised eyebrow. His eyes are pits of nothingness, just pure black. As I take in his face, I think fleetingly of our old world and the likes of Matt Bomer.

Only, this guy is no pampered actor. He's a warrior, and his onyx-black eyes are fixed on me. There's nothing friendly about the way he looks at me, either. I get the gut-churning feeling he's about to skin me alive.

Printed in Great Britain
by Amazon

80366967R00109